**THE RO**

As for Sarah, she could only remember the low
caressing tones of Philippe Cadot's voice. The
implication of his words could not be mistaken,
and their meaning was flattering to a woman
who'd been married since she was seventeen.

She could not help seeing the expression on his
handsome face; it reminded her of Tam, in the
old days, when he had come courting her. And
what a long time ago that seemed, on this sparkling
day, and how easily he'd developed into the
shouting, ranting, pompous Tam of today . . .

She sighed a little, forgetting how she had boasted
of her contentment with her lot barely an hour ago,
when Melissa had laughed at her and told her to
take care, or the gods might be listening.

# The Romantic Frenchman

# Mary Ann Gibbs

**CORONET BOOKS**
Hodder Paperbacks Ltd., London

Copyright © 1967 by Mary Ann Gibbs
First published 1967 by Hurst and
Blackett Ltd., London
Coronet edition 1975

Printed and bound in Great Britain for
Coronet Books, Hodder Paperbacks Ltd,
St. Paul's House, Warwick Lane,
London, EC4P 4AH
by Hunt Barnard Printing Ltd,
Aylesbury, Bucks.

ISBN 0 340 18985 1

# I

'You may say what you like, Henrietta,' said her sister Charity from her seat in the bow window of her little house that overlooked Doverton High Street, 'but reading between the lines of Miss Rebecca Prestwick's letter it is quite plain to me that poor Mel has been jilted, and no girl of spirit likes being jilted, especially when her father happens to be Rector of a parish so full of spiteful young ladies as Brinkford Parva appears to be.'

'All parishes are full of spiteful young ladies,' said the Dowager Lady Tamporley calmly. 'And spiteful old ones as well when the Rector's daughter is as pretty as Melissa. But as Mel's aunt has not said that the child was ever engaged to this man, and in fact has told us nothing about him beyond the fact that he is rich and good-looking, I cannot see how you can say that she has been jilted. And what is his name, pray? Do we know even that about him?'

'I'm afraid not, dear,' said Miss Cheriton, rightly translating the pronoun as being used in the royal sense. 'And maybe there was no actual engagement between them, but Rebecca seems to think that he was very much attracted to Mel, and he paid her so much attention that what with him being so wealthy, and everybody's eye being on him as it were, an engagement was talked about everywhere, and in fact hourly expected, when he suddenly left the district.'

'And has not been seen near it since,' said the Dowager disparagingly. 'So much for his devotion to Mel! A great many wealthy men are attracted to pretty girls without falling in love sufficiently to want to marry them. And from my knowledge of Rebecca Prestwick I have no doubt that she has exaggerated the whole thing.'

'All the same she does say in her letter that Mel looks peaky and she would like the child to have a change of air,' said Miss Charity pensively. The Dowager said nothing, and after a moment her sister continued perseveringly, 'Brinkford Parva is very relaxing: I found it so myself when I used to go and visit there when dearest Bella was alive.'

'It is quite impossible for me to have Mel to stay with me just now,' said the Dowager firmly.

'Then I shall have her,' said Miss Cheriton with an angry toss of her head. 'There is always room for her in *my* house, small as it is, and if the man has behaved as badly as Rebecca says he has then I will invite some of our charming French officers to come and help me to console her.' And she glanced at the street below the window as if looking for some such consolation herself.

'Ask her to stay by all means,' said the Dowager placidly. 'It will be company for you, my dear. But I should not encourage too great an interest in our French officers if I were you, Charity. From what I hear of these young foreigners they are over-willing to console English girls these days, especially if they should be feeling slighted by somebody else and more than ready to be consoled.'

'As you do not entertain any of the French officers up at Tamporley as we do in the town here, Henrietta,' said Miss Cheriton in some excitement, 'I don't see how you can know what they are like!'

'But you know how I am placed at the Dower House, dear.' The Dowager never allowed herself to become excited about anything. 'Not only is Tamporley out of bounds to the prisoners at the Castle, but we have an old French émigré living almost at our gate. Even if we were within the required boundary for the officers out on parole, I could not insult the Comte d'Estoban by asking him to dine at my house with officers of Bonaparte's army!'

Miss Cheriton realised that her sister had adroitly introduced another controversial subject in order to avoid any more discussion of Mel's affairs and she was justly indignant. She could not help rising to the bait however.

'There can't be any necessity for you to invite French officers on the same day as you ask the Comte to dinner,' she pointed out. 'And in any case I am sure he would not mind. He is a singularly gentle old man.'

The Dowager said that she would not dream of subjecting him to such an ordeal all the same and added in her sleepy way, 'And then, you see, there's Tam . . . '

'Ah yes, *Tam*!' agreed Miss Cheriton significantly. 'That's far more the root of the matter!'

Her nephew, Sir Tamporley Brevitt Tamporley, had a hearty British dislike for all foreigners, were they French, Dutch, Danish or American, and in its time Doverton Castle had housed war prisoners from many countries. Fortunately Tamporley Park and the village were some way outside the town, and the mile-stone that marked the boundary of the officers out on parole fell quite a long way short of them.

Miss Cheriton saw her sister's face exhibit a mild displeasure at the implied criticism of Tam and returned rather unkindly to Mel. 'I am sure Sarah will insist on having her to stay when she knows what has happened,' she said. 'They are devoted to each other, and the children adore her.'

'I daresay Sarah will have her to stay as long as she will promise not to interfere with the children's lessons as much as she did last time. She will find Miss Pope a great deal less easy than little Miss Davis, while as for Mrs. Forsett . . . ' Here words failed the Dowager and Miss Cheriton's vexation left her as she exchanged an understanding smile with her sister.

Sarah Tamporley, never very strong, had found it hard to recover from the birth of her youngest child, James, and her mother, a strong-minded lady with firm ideas on the upbringing of the young, had declared the care of five high-spirited children to be a task completely beyond her daughter's powers. She had moved into Tamporley Park and taken up her residence there, and although James was now three years old, she had not left it for more than a day or so since.

The first thing she did was to dismiss pretty little Miss Davis and to engage a strict lady of uncertain years and sour countenance to instil discipline into the unruly band, remarking to her son-in-law that only thus could she prevent his children from becoming utterly spoiled. For what their mother started at the Park was continued recklessly and with total disregard for the formation of their characters and manners by the Dowager at the Dower House and their Great-Aunt Charity in the town, and in order to further this excellent work she insisted on the learning of the Multiplication Table and Latin verbs before breakfast.

Miss Charity, to whom figures of any sort were a nightmare, and with a vivid recollection of her own struggles with Latin verbs in the days of her youth, held the opinion that to inflict such things on young children on empty stomachs amounted to sadistic torture, and she did not hesitate to tell her nephew so though he only laughed at her for her pains.

'I daresay Mel will get around Miss Pope all the same,' said Melissa's Aunt Charity with unfounded optimism. 'I know she will like her, in spite of being such a dragon, and dear Sarah always lets Mel do exactly as she pleases.'

'Sarah lets everybody do exactly as they please,' said young Lady Tamporley's mother-in-law plaintively. 'But I am afraid Melissa won't get round Mrs. Forsett so easily. The last time Mel was staying with me at the Dower House Mrs. Forsett said she had never known anybody who could make the children so undisciplined and ill-mannered in so short a time.'

'Mel was only a child herself then, but she is nineteen now, and I daresay she is a great deal more grown-up,' said Charity smiling.

Her sister admitted that she was very fond of Melissa. 'I only wish that Sarah had some of her spirit,' she added with a sigh. 'But she is always ailing, poor girl . . . It is very hard on Tam to have a wife who is for ever falling ill.'

'But she is very pretty, dear, and her ill-health gives her quite a transparent look – like a piece of porcelain . . . Poor dear Sarah! She will be imposed on all her life.' And then she had to abandon the subject as the parlour door opened and Miss Cheriton's little maid, Patty, showed Sarah's husband into the room.

Tamporley Brevitt Tamporley was a fine young man of thirty, with the red complexion of one who is out in the air, whatever the weather, and the muscular frame of a man who is as ready to wield an axe with one of his foresters as to help his grooms to break in a colt for his stables. It was a never failing source of wonder to Miss Cheriton that a superbly healthy man like Tam should have selected the fragile Sarah for his wife.

'I saw Mamma's carriage at your door,' he said, kissing his aunt. 'And so I called to ask if Dickson had been to see you yet about the repairs to your house?'

'Not yet, dear, but I have no doubt that he will.' Miss Cheriton liked her nephew's bailiff, a pleasant, agreeable gentleman who could sometimes be persuaded to take a glass of wine with her in the morning-room when he called to discuss leaking cisterns and peeling wall-paper.

'Be sure to remind him about the roof. I did mention it to him but he may forget, and I want him to see that everything is put in order for you, Aunt Charity.'

'The winter gales stripped the lead in one place only,' said his aunt. 'And the water comes in very little, and in an attic that we don't use. But I will remind him about it to be sure.' She smiled at her large nephew with affection. 'We were talking about Mel,' she added.

9

'Sarah also had a letter from Miss Rebecca.' He laughed, but his eyes were as shrewd as his mother's. 'She appears to be anxious for her to have a change of air.'

'And quite properly too,' said Miss Charity sharply. 'The child has plenty of relatives who are well able to entertain her. I was telling your mother just now that I am going to have her, and that I will invite some of our French officers in to amuse her, and I am sure that dear Sarah will be equally happy to have her to stay with you at the Park.'

'Oh, you know Sarah! She had not got half way through Miss Rebecca's letter before she was ready to have Mel for six months or more, but I would rather that your Frenchmen entertained her if you have no objections, Aunt'

'It's Mrs. Forsett, I suppose,' said Miss Cheriton in disgust. 'She has put her foot on the whole project.'

Tam laughed.

'Well, I must admit, Aunt Charity, I don't see why my household should be set in an uproar and my children made unmanageable and their lessons upset because my cousin has a broken heart.'

'Then you are very unkind, Tam!' cried Miss Charity.

'On the contrary, Sarah and I have great affection for Mel, but she is a sad flirt, and I daresay this fellow - whoever he may be - was frightened off by her irresponsible conduct.'

'Now you are being pompous, Tam!'

'I am not being pompous. I told Mel to her face the last time we met that no man of sense would tie himself for life to a flirt, and this has proved that I was right, though she did laugh at me for my advice.'

'Mel has always laughed at you, Tam dear!' said Miss Cheriton maliciously. 'It does you good.'

'I will not take you up on that, but I find it extremely irritating, to say the least of it, and when she was last at Tamporley she quarrelled with me so incessantly that on more than one occasion Mrs. Forsett had to lecture her on her manners, and poor Sarah was so upset that she took to her bed.'

'I will warn Mel to be careful how she behaves this time,' said his aunt.

'I hope you will,' said Tam, and with this parting shot he went back to his phaeton and the spirited young bay that the groom was holding in with difficulty some distance behind the Dowager's carriage.

'Poor Sarah is such a gentle little creature,' sighed Tam's mother indulgently. 'Anything in the nature of a scene upsets her.'

Miss Cheriton could understand it. When her nephew was contradicted or crossed so that he lost his temper, he would begin to shout, and on such occasions she too had felt sometimes that she would like to take to her bed. She said indignantly that she would keep Mel away from Tamporley during the whole of her visit. 'None of her relatives need clap eyes on the poor girl,' she added, her voice rising hysterically.

'Compose yourself, my dear,' said the Dowager sensibly. 'You know quite well that we shall all be happy to see dear Mel at all times while she is with you. It is simply not convenient for me – or for Sarah – to have her to stay.'

'I have noticed,' said Miss Cheriton, not attempting to compose herself, 'that people who have large houses seldom do find it convenient to have their poorer relations to stay.'

The Dowager said she thought she had better be getting home, or she would be late for dinner, and Mrs. Slater would not like that at all. 'You may be thankful, Charity,' she added with mild benevolence, 'that you have not got a housekeeper to consider! I am sure your Patty is much easier to please!'

*     *     *

In her reply to her aunt's invitation Melissa said that she would be delighted to see Doverton again.

*Tell the children at Tamporley that I am bringing a new game of Chance with me,* she wrote. *It is a said gamble, so perhaps we had better only play it when they visit us at your house. I feel that Tam's charming mother-in-law would look on it with stern disapproval, but when she is not by we will wager our counters on each throw of the dice and enjoy ourselves to our hearts' content.* She added that she would be happy to make the acquaintance of some of the Frenchmen at the Castle. *Is M. Cadot still there, or has he broken his parole so many times that he has been sent off to Edinburgh or Dartmoor as a punishment? Poor Lieutenant Cadot, he and I had so much in common. He could never be serious over discipline and neither could I! And how handsome he was to be sure. Do you remember how I used to call him your Romantic Frenchman?*

The days went by, the first of March came, and with it Melissa, on the London mail because the Rector's stipend could not stretch to posting for his daughter – a Melissa moreover who, in the eyes of her fond aunt, looked prettier than ever. There was a carmine feather in her grey bonnet, and her dark eyes sparkled with pleasure at seeing Miss Cheriton again. They left her boxes at the Coach office to be sent later and walked up the hill together to her aunt's little house at the top of the High Street, rather than take one of the dilapidated hackney cabs that waited there.

'I don't like your Doverton hackney cabs,' Mel said laughing. 'The last time I took one I caught fleas!' She tucked her hand into her aunt's arm. 'Dear little Doverton!' she said affectionately. 'It never alters.'

Her aunt asked after Miss Rebecca Prestwick, who had come to keep house for her brother when his wife Bella died after Melissa was born. She was a careful woman, with little sense of humour and a cheese-paring nature, but Miss Cheriton was the first to admit that she had looked after the Rector and his daughter well and with affection. 'I suppose she was

12

much put out over this unfortunate love affair of yours, dear?' she added mournfully.

Melissa laughed a little self-consciously. 'Oh, from the way Aunt Rebecca went on you might have thought that he had been paying his addresses to her instead of to me!' she said.

Miss Cheriton met the laughing eyes gravely and with some misgiving. 'It is scarcely a matter for frivolity, my dear!' she said. 'I did not realise from Rebecca's letter that the man was really serious!'

'Oh yes!' Melissa's voice was purposely cool. 'He asked me to marry him.'

'He asked you' . . . Her aunt was really startled now. 'I had no idea that he had gone as far as that, Mel!'

'And I refused him,' continued Melissa calmly.

Here Miss Cheriton could find no words, and then she uttered the first that came to her mind. 'But . . . didn't you like him, Mel?'

'Very much.'

'And Rebecca said that he was handsome ; ; ; and rich, dear!'

'Yes. He was, I think, as handsome as your romantic Frenchman, Aunt Charity, and his income is reputed to be in the region of seven thousand a year, with an estate in Norfolk.'

'And you refused him? But *why*, Mel?' Miss Cheriton's rising voice held nothing but grief for her niece's folly.

'Because he took me for granted,' said Melissa petulantly. 'He didn't even ask Papa's permission first. He met me as I was out walking with Pom in the lane and before I knew what he was at he had hold of my hand and was asking me to marry him. I was very angry with him.'

'But my dearest Mel, it sounds as if the poor fellow's feelings had run away with him . . .'

'Pom's feelings ran away with him too. He bit him.'

'Poor man! No wonder he left the district!'

13

'Yes. I'm afraid Pom and I gave his proposal a poor reception.'

'And you do not regret it?' Miss Cheriton could not quite keep a note of reproach out of her voice.

'Not in the least.' Melissa saw the doubt in Miss Cheriton's face and laughed wryly. 'Oh well, sometimes I wonder if I were not perhaps rather foolish. I'm not likely to get such a good offer again. I suppose the truth of the matter was,' she went on after a moment, 'that I only encouraged him because my bosom friend, Emily Clarke, said that he would never offer for me and I wanted to prove that she was wrong – horrid thing. But when he did offer, you see, I was so taken aback that I did not know what to do, and I had to refuse him because if I had accepted him I'd have been forced to throw him over in the end, which would have been even more shocking. I had reached an impasse!'

'And what did Miss Emily Clarke say when you told her?'

'Oh, she said I was making it all up and that he hadn't proposed to me at all, because if he had he would have asked Papa first and Aunt Rebecca would have known and it would have been all over the neighbourhood by that time    . And she was right of course,' said Melissa mournfully. 'I could have scratched her eyes out.'

'And you have had no more offers, my dear?'

'Not unless you count the one I had from Frank Woodcock when I was sixteen and staying at Tamporley.'

'An ensign in the militia! Oh Mel!'

'Well, I daresay he is a Captain now and just as charming and penniless.'

'Oh yes, dear, he is.'

'Well then I'm glad I did not have him. We'd have spent our married life in and out of debtors' prisons.'

'Mel, don't say such dreadful things!'

'Dearest Aunt Charity. It is so easy to shock you. Tell me how is my darling Sarah? And is Tam still under the thumb of Dragon Forsett?'

'Not quite as much as he was, in fact I have seen distinct signs of rebellion in Tam just lately, and I believe it would not take much for him to send her packing.'

'Then I hope he does it soon. I dislike Mrs. Forsett as dearly as I love her daughter. I wonder that Tam has not quarrelled with her long ago, but there is only one person with whom he quarrels, and that's me.'

'Indeed yes!' sighed Miss Cheriton.

'He likes his own way too much,' explained Melissa. 'And I like mine. It is only natural that we should quarrel when we meet.'

'Then I wish you did not because it does not make for harmony in a family.'

'But we mean nothing by it, in fact as far as Tam's concerned I am the leaven in a lump of dough.'

'Now that is going too far. I must protest against you calling poor Tam a lump of dough!'

'I beg your pardon, Aunt Charity. Tam is a nice, good creature, if nature has endowed him with less than the average share of brains. I am sure he has the kindest heart – and the loudest voice – in the universe.' And then they arrived at Miss Cheriton's house to find the Tamporley curricle drawing up outside it and Sarah seated in it beside her husband with a basket of wild daffodils on her knees.

'I have been instructed to bring you these, Mel!' Sarah cried, as the groom took the basket from her and helped her to alight, and she kissed her cousin warmly. 'Welcome to Doverton, my dearest! The children were so wild with excitement when they heard that you were coming today that Miss Pope took them into the park, so that they could work off their high spirits in gathering daffodils especially for you!'

'I hope you appreciate the honour that is done you, Mel!' added her husband in a voice that could have been heard in the market-place.

'But of course I do.' Melissa smiled delightedly at them. 'Give the children my love and tell them that I will be at

15

the Park to see them the first morning that I am free.' And then she caught sight of a young man who had stopped as he was passing the house and was staring at the daffodils and Sarah's sweet face above them as if he were an artist, trying to paint a picture on his mind so that he could remember it for ever. 'Aunt Charity!' she cried. 'Do you see who is here? . . . Your Romantic Frenchman!' And she stepped forward quickly and held out her hand. 'Monsieur Cadot!' she said warmly. 'So you have not been sent away after all!'

Tamporley stared in astonishment and his wife in smiling amusement as the young man, whose sallow complexion and shabby coat proclaimed him to be one of the French officers from the Castle, took the hand she held out to him and raised it to his lips.

'Mademoiselle Melissa!' he said gallantly. 'Your aunt told me that you were to come back to Doverton to visit us again.' But although his smiles were for Melissa his eyes still dwelt on Sarah and the basket of daffodils she was holding. 'I was walking down this hill saying to myself how I detested the long, cold English spring, and suddenly I hear a voice like music, and the winter in my heart is ended . . . Your servant, Mademoiselle Melissa! . . . Your servant, Mademoiselle Cheriton!'

'If he bows much lower,' thought Tamporley, disgusted, 'he'll crack his head on the pavement!' His aunt introduced Sarah and her husband to the Frenchman and he bowed again, as low as before, and said that he was enchanted, while Tam looked anything but enchanted. He glared at the Lieutenant, and if he had had a poker thrust down his back his answering bow could not have been slighter in acknowledging the other's politeness. And then the Lieutenant stood upright and the eyes of the two men met.

'But we have met before, I think!' said the Frenchman, astonished.

Melissa, glancing at her cousin, was surprised to see a dark flush spread over his face and she was quite sure that he too

16

had recognised the Lieutenant, but all he said was that he was mistaken. 'Never seen you before in my life, sir,' he declared.

'If you say so, Monsieur.' The Frenchman's smile was mechanically polite, but his eyes went back to Sarah and the daffodils as if she drew them irresistibly.

'I do say so, sir!' shouted Sir Tamporley Brevitt Tamporley, and without moderating his voice told his wife that it was time they went home as he couldn't hold his animals in much longer. The pair in the curricle were only a year older than the bay that he drove in the phaeton and were showing decided signs of restiveness, and Sarah apologised for keeping them waiting.

'Allow me, Madame.' The Frenchman took the basket from her and slipped in front of the groom to hand her into the carriage. She smiled her thanks while Tam rewarded him with a glare for his officiousness, and then he stepped back and stood bare-headed as the groom sprang up behind and the curricle moved off up the street.

'Prancing, frog-eating, insufferable monkey!' growled Tam. 'Aunt Charity's Romantic Frenchman indeed! I don't see anything romantic about *him*!'

Young Lady Tamporley said nothing. The smile was still on her lips and it stayed there, even when Tam drove the curricle at such speed back to Tamporley that he nearly overturned it at the bridge over the river, and the hens outside the Tamporley Arms scattered squawking as if a fox had got among them.

# 2

It was well-known in Doverton that Sir Tamporley Brevitt Tamporley's father, Sir Humphrey, had been a shy and unobtrusive philanthropist, and one of the many kindly acts he did was to buy Miss Cheriton's house in the High Street and leave it to her in his will, with the proviso that the expense of all repairs should be borne by his son.

It was a stoutly-built little house, about fifty years old, of white stone with a flight of steps up to the front door and an elegant fanlight above. On either side of this door small bow windows looked out over the street and the area, and above the bow windows four sash windows, in pairs, one above the other, followed suit. It was a neat little house, as neat as its owner, and Miss Cheriton was very happy there. Not only was her only surviving sister living at the Dower House at Tamporley, but the village was less than a mile and half away from the top of the High Street, and on a fine morning it made a pleasant walk, while in dirty weather the Dowager would send her carriage when she felt herself to be in need of her sister's company.

In Doverton itself there were a number of ladies of Miss Cheriton's age, either spinsters or widows, all living on slender means and ready and willing to come and spend an evening with her, playing cards, or to invite her to their houses to listen to a little music or partake of a frugal meal.

On these occasions their conversation was usually enlivened with stories and anecdotes about the French officer prisoners of war either living at the Castle, or in lodgings in the town, and whose charming manners and friendly ways had made a colourful addition to their society.

Miss Cheriton was assiduous in taking her niece to pay her usual courtesy morning calls on all her friends, and it was a few days before Melissa found a free morning in which to walk to Tamporley to thank the children for the daffodils. The post was in long before she came down to breakfast that morning: she had heard the horn sounding in the streets as she dressed and they had scarcely finished breakfast when the postman arrived with the letters. There was one for her from her father, in which the Rector related the more amusing items of gossip in the parish, said that he hoped she would enjoy her stay, and that Pom missed her very much and so did he. She did not know how keenly she had expected some item of news, however small, about Edward Beaumont until she found herself reading the letter through a second time with anxiety, in case there was something that she had overlooked. But after all why should the Rector mention him? His acquaintance with Mr. Beaumont had been of the slightest description.

It was too fine a morning however to allow herself to be teased by thoughts of Edward Beaumont, and feeling that by this time there could not be many of her aunt's friends in Doverton who did not know that she was among them, she asked her if she would have any objection if she walked over to Tamporley that morning.

'It will do you good, my love,' said her aunt, who was longing to discuss Melissa and her love affair with her acquaintances and only sorry that she still did not know the young man's name. 'And if any friends should come – to return your calls you know – I will tell them that you have gone to pay your respects to your cousins.' Miss Cheriton's friends basked as she did in the reflected glory of the Park.

To Melissa, who had spent many happy visits at the Park when she was a child, there was nothing at all awe-inspiring about the place. It was large, certainly, but there was scarcely a yard of it with which she was not as well acquainted as she was with the Rectory at home, and she set out impatiently, glad when the town was left behind and the country road lay before her, the March wind whipping the hair from under her bonnet and the colour into her cheeks. As she climbed the stile that led to the short cut across the park to the house, she felt her father's letter crackle in her pocket and the sunshine of the day dimmed a little and the wind seemed colder and more penetrating.

She thought again of Edward Beaumont and the look in his eyes when he had at last understood that she had only been playing with him. To a man of his position and dignity it must have been an intolerable moment, and she wished most heartily that she had never set eyes on the odious Miss Emily Clarke, and that she had not been so eager to encourage him nor so ready to refuse him when the moment came. Because although she had been ready to laugh about it with her Aunt Charity she was secretly very much ashamed of her part in the affair.

She had traversed the path that led up through the park and across the stream behind the Comte d'Estoban's cottage and had reached the shelter of a small coppice beyond when she saw her cousin Tamporley coming towards her, and her feeling of regret for her behaviour to Mr. Beaumont made her greet him more kindly than usual.

'Why is it,' she asked as he turned and walked a little way towards the house beside her, 'that as one grows older one finds it is one's follies, rather than one's sins, that one regrets the most?'

Tamporley said with truth that it was a situation in which he seldom found himself. 'And while we are on the subject of folly, my dear Mel,' he added, 'I want a word with you if you please.'

'Oh dear!' Her glance was half-dismayed, half-droll. 'When you say it in that tone of voice I know I am in for many words and on a subject that I shall not like. But I've been in Doverton for less than a week, Tam, so that I don't see what you can have to scold me about this time.'

'I was not going to scold you,' he replied with dignity, his voice rising. 'I was merely going to give you a cousinly word of warning. I know that Aunt Charity is very fond of certain people in the town, but I have never thought her to be particularly wise in her choice of friends, and I would ask you to be careful, Mel. In other words, if I were you, I would not encourage her friends among the French officers from the Castle.'

The smile faded from Melissa's face. 'Now why do you say that?' she asked mildly.

'Well . . . ' He hesitated. 'These Frenchies have friends in Doverton who could not possibly be introduced to any lady from Tamporley Park.'

'I don't understand you, Tam.' She frowned at him. 'What sort of friends have these French officers that you should dislike them so much? Do you mean among the tradespeople, or something of that sort?'

'Exactly.' He was almost too eager to agree with her. 'That is precisely what I meant, Mel. They are, in fact, a very bourgeois sort of men, these French officers, and I am afraid there are few gentlemen among them.'

'Bourgeois.' Her frown deepened. 'I've always wondered what that word meant. The Comte uses it sometimes doesn't he? What *does* it mean, Tam?'

He thought she was laughing at him again and his temper began to rise. 'It means that they move in circles that your father would not like you to mix in, Melissa.'

'But he likes me to mix with all sorts of people!' she protested. 'He says that nobody can know his or her fellow human beings if he keeps rigidly to his own class.'

'Don't argue with me, Melissa!' His voice rose rapidly with his sense of exasperation. 'I wish you would not twist my words to suit yourself. It is an irritating habit that I hoped

21

you would overcome as you grow older, but I see you have not done it yet.'

'I am sorry, Tam.' She remembered her promise to her Aunt Charity not to quarrel with him. 'But you should not be so illogical, dear!' He did not reply, striding on in offended dignity, and she added after a moment, 'How is dearest Sarah?'

'Dearest Sarah is proposing to visit Briggs's shop in Doverton this morning. It seems that Briggs has a consignment of new French silks that he would like her to see, and my mother is going with her.'

'French silks? With a war raging between our two countries?'

'No doubt Briggs has his smugglers like everyone else. The brandy my fellow brings me is certainly from France.'

'And will Mrs. Forsett be accompanying us?'

'Mrs. Forsett left Tamporley this morning.'

'No!' Melissa felt her spirits rise delightfully. 'For how long?'

'She is not certain.' His good temper had returned however as he gave the information and the smile that accompanied it was so broad that she guessed his pleasure to be as great as her own. 'She has gone to stay with her brother-in-law Squire Forsett, at Dove Tye.'

Melissa congratulated him on having rid himself of the lady and wondered what had persuaded her to leave Tamporley, which was infinitely larger and more comfortable, besides being set in far prettier country, than her brother-in-law's draughty old Manor House in the low-lying marshes on the far side of Doverton. As Tam did not seem able to enlighten her on the subject she knew she would have to wait until she saw Sarah before satisfying her curiosity, and she asked brightly how the children were progressing under Miss Pope. 'I was sorry when little Miss Davis left,' she added. 'She was so pretty and she laughed a lot. I think laughter and pretty people must be a great deal better for children than crossness and sour looks.'

'Miss Davis had no control over the children at all. That was why she left.'

'Excuse me, Tam, but that was not the reason I was given for her dismissal. Mrs. Forsett said she was setting her cap at the French officers!' She glanced wickedly at her cousin's face and saw a slow grin spread over his features. 'What a good thing I shall not see Mrs. Forsett while I'm here this time. She might accuse *me* of setting my cap at them too!'

'It would be little use if you did.' Good-naturedly he refused to be drawn into further argument. 'They are not seriously interested in young ladies with no fortunes.'

'Yet they pay one such charming compliments!'

'Which they do not mean in the least.'

'But what does it matter if they mean a compliment or not as long as it is delightful to hear?'

'That, Mel, is a most worldly sentiment for a Rector's daughter!'

They both laughed and she reminded him that she was not a Rector's daughter from choice, but that it was a walk in life that had been thrust upon her, and then, as the house came in sight and she saw Sarah's carriage waiting, they parted, Tam to go on to the stables and Melissa to join his wife.

Nothing could have revealed Mrs. Forsett's absence so much as the presence of the children on the terrace with their mother; they bowled their hoops and skipped with their skipping ropes and raced each other and came back to her to throw their arms round her waist, demanding her attention for a dozen things at once as she took a few turns there in the sunshine, protected by the Great House from the wind. Melissa picked up her skirts and ran across the grass and the intervening gravel walk and up the stone steps between its big stone vases to join them, and she was delighted to observe that three years of Mrs. Forsett's rule had not managed to subdue Sarah's children in the least.

As soon as they saw her they came to her like birds in

flight, racing across the terrace and down the steps and having reached her they flung themselves upon her. She was immediately hidden in arms that hugged, in capering figures, in frenzied delight: her bonnet was tipped off and her arms were extended to enfold and embrace.

Watching them for a moment Tamporley smiled rather ruefully as he remembered his mother-in-law's remarks about the effect his cousin had on his children, and then as his gentle little wife joined her embraces to theirs he turned on his heel and went off to the stables.

'Women!' he thought with a shrug of his shoulders as he went. 'They are all the same!'

But they were not all the same of course. There was his mother, the Dowager, placid and indolent, and his Aunt Charity, fluttering about him like a frightened hen, and his mother-in-law, hard as granite and with no thought but her own wishes and her own comfort. And there was Sarah, who went white when he shouted at her, and Melissa, who went red and shouted at him back. And he did not know which of the five he found most exasperating. So he went on to the stables and shouted at the groom there to have the phaeton ready for him in fifteen minutes' time, and it relieved his feelings a lot, because although the groom did not go white or look at all frightened, neither did he answer him back. He knew he would lose his place if he did.

\*　　\*　　\*

The children were sent back to their lessons while Sarah took Melissa's arm and led her round to the waiting carriage.

'I am so glad you have come, Mel dearest,' she said. 'Now you can help us to choose our new dresses. Your taste is so much better than mine. That grey bonnet and the carmine feather suit you very well . . . though it needs to be put straight I think!'

'The children knocked it off,' said Melissa. She put the bonnet on again, tying the ribbons under her chin.

'I am glad Mamma was not here to see them,' said Sarah. 'She does not like to see them so rough, though I try to tell her that it is only their high spirits . . . playful darlings, as Aunt Charity calls them!'

Melissa asked if any of the playful darlings would be accompanying them.

'Oh no!' Sarah was shocked. 'They have wasted half an hour with me as it is, but I rather think Miss Pope was relieved to say goodbye to Mamma for a time. Her discipline is not quite so unsparing when Mamma is not by, and I noticed that the Multiplication Tables had been postponed this morning until after breakfast. We were all so relieved!'

'Tam says Mrs. Forsett has gone to your uncle's house at Dove Tye.'

'Yes. It was because of poor Sophy, you see.'

'Sophy?' For a moment Melissa was puzzled and then recollection came: she had met Squire Forsett's only child when she was at Tamporley three years ago. At that time Sophy Forsett had been a disastrously plain girl, but with a large fortune to inherit from an old uncle when she reached the age of twenty-one. Melissa had envied her the fortune, but not her looks. 'Is she as plain as ever?' she asked.

'Worse,' said Sarah unhappily. 'And it makes it so difficult for Mamma and poor Uncle William.' As Melissa said nothing but looked at her questioningly she went on, 'It's the fortune hunters, Mel.'

They had reached the carriage by this time and when they were inside it with the fur rug over their knees, and the horses moving off towards the avenue, Melissa asked her what she meant. 'What fortune hunters?' she wanted to know.

Sarah hesitated. 'Sophy will be twenty-one at the beginning of April,' she said then. 'And nobody would ever dream of marrying her for her looks, Mel. She has the face of a good-natured horse . . . and she *is* good-natured! In fact I think she is one of the nicest-natured girls that I know. But being so rich attracts a number of undesirable young men to her, and Mamma and Uncle William have been kept in a continual state of alarm and anxiety over the last few months in case she should set her heart on marrying one of these young wastrels. Tam says it is all a lot of rubbish and she should be allowed to choose for herself, but of course it would be a terrible thing if poor Sophy married in haste and spent the rest of her life regretting it.'

'But surely she is sensible enough to know when a man is only after her money?' protested Melissa. 'She did not strike me as being a stupid girl when I met her.'

The glance that Sarah gave her was full of wisdom. 'Would you want to believe that a young man was only after your money, if you were in her shoes?' she asked.

'Well no, I might not *want* to believe it,' agreed Melissa. 'Is that why your mother has gone to Dove Tye, because one of these horrid young men is promising to be successful in his pursuit of Sophy?'

'Oh no. It is quite the opposite this time.' Sarah smiled. 'There's a man who is coming to stay with the Halsteads at Dove Tye Hall. He is a friend of theirs and he met Sophy at a ball in London a few weeks ago, and he wrote to Mr. Halstead asking if he could visit him, and Mrs. Halstead says he is certain that he was very taken with poor Sophy and wants to follow up the acquaintance.'

'I see. But why shouldn't your mother think that he may be after Sophy's money too?'

'Because, my dearest Mel, he has plenty of his own! And Mrs. Halstead told Mamma that the poor man had been so badly treated by a very pretty girl after Christmas that she thinks he has taken a dislike to all pretty faces in consequence, and that is why he is so attracted to Sophy!'

Melissa agreed that it looked promising. 'Do you know his name?' she added.

'No . . . At least, if I did I have forgotten it. But it's of no consequence, as he is a nice man and really in love with Sophy. The Halsteads are quite set up by it all. They have had so much trouble with that naughty boy Edwin.'

'I thought he had purchased a commission in one of the Foot regiments?'

'He did intend to, and indeed for a time he talked quite seriously about it, and was even measured for his uniform and his sword, and then it all came to nothing . . . He is at home now, driving about the countryside in a dreadful new phaeton with a quite unmanageable horse that nobody else would buy, because it kicks everything to bits, knocking down peoples' gate-posts and driving old women into the gutter . . Tam says he'll either break his neck or find himself in gaol, and that he'd do either for him himself with the greatest pleasure.'

Melissa laughed and said that young Edwin Halstead was probably very good for the neighbourhood. 'While as for you, Sarah, my love, you are more beautiful than ever. But then you never alter. You are always the same gentle unruffled creature, and lovely to look at. I saw Aunt Charity's Romantic Frenchman gazing at you as if you were a being from another world. Do you ever lose your temper, Sarah?'

Sarah laughed and blushed. 'I try not to,' she said.

'And I shouldn't think it needs a great effort on your part either. I wish I were more like you, but I do and say such stupid things and then I'm sorry, and being sorry is no use because it won't undo or unsay what you have said and done.'

'Oh Mel, you are nineteen now, and still you have not grown up!'

'Don't talk as if you were all that much older than I am, Sarah. There are only seven years between us.'

'Ah yes, but then you see I was married at seventeen, and I grew up quickly.' Sarah's face was suddenly subdued and it occurred to Melissa that five children and a husband like Tam might have an ageing effect on a woman. Then young Lady Tamporley smiled, and her smooth brow and her blue eyes were as serene as ever. 'I really am one of the most fortunate women on earth,' she said. 'I wish you could have my luck, Mel!'

The wind met them, cold and chilling, as the carriage came out of the sheltered avenue on to the road across the open park land and Melissa shivered suddenly and put up the window. 'Don't say such things without touching wood, Sarah!' she cried. 'The gods may be listening!'

'Let them listen!' Sarah laughed teasingly. 'Dearest Mel! Still thinking about your innocent little sins and follies! . . . Let us think about our new silk dresses instead!' After a moment she went on, 'It's almost time for the wild violets to be out in the coppice above the Comte's little house. If it is as fine as this tomorrow you must come and spend the day with me, and we'll walk down through the park and explore all our old haunts together, and we'll pick wild daffodils and violets for M. Estoban, because he does love flowers in his rooms, and that sour old Frenchwoman who looks after him will grow nothing but vegetables in his little patch of garden.'

But Melissa was not listening. She was thinking of Sophy's admirer, and of another man who had gone courting a pretty girl at Christmas-time, and she wondered if Mr. Beaumont too had lost his liking for pretty faces . . .

# 3

The carriage made its way towards the East gates, where old Mrs. Baines came out to open them and drop a curtsey, and on to the Dower House where the Dowager joined them, sitting with Sarah facing the horses while Melissa settled herself happily opposite them, and they went on down the main road to Doverton because the road that led down to the market square was better than the one into the High Street.

The morning was cold but still lovely and the park that followed the road, with the Heath on the other side, was beautiful, with its drifts of bright green where new grass was springing up into the winter brown, and the sloe blossom white over dark clusters of bramble and gorse.

March was an exciting month, thought Sarah, looking out of her window in contentment. Things were stirring under the earth and the sap was beginning to rise. In no time at all April would be there and a wayward warmth would spread through the land, with summer just ahead. True, English summers were seldom as lovely as one expected they would be, but one always lived in hope that they would come up to expectation before autumn closed in again.

The horses moved briskly and the Dowager talked about Miss Pope and the children, and told Sarah what should be done now that Mrs. Forsett was not there, and as Sarah agreed with her smilingly and went on looking out of her window, she turned to Melissa to ask her what colour she should choose for her new silk dress.

29

'Purple,' she suggested. 'Or do you think a nice bottle green would suit me best?'

Melissa exclaimed in horror. 'Maize or pale blue,' she declared.

'With black lace,' added Sarah turning from her contemplation of the March day to yield a concession to the Dowager's fifty-two years.

'Maize or pale blue?' exclaimed her mother-in-law. 'At my time of life?'

'Why should you not wear pretty colours?' demanded Melissa. 'You, a very handsome lady in the prime of life!'

'You are a pair of flatterers!' proclaimed the Dowager but her smiles told them that she liked it.

The carriage came down the cobbled streets of the town and even the grim pile of the Castle that dominated it on the opposite hill had a kinder aspect in the sun. They turned to the right and climbed the hill to Market Street and into the March wind that blew down it, and the coachman brought the carriage to a standstill in front of Mr. Briggs's shop, which seemed to stock everything that anybody could need. The groom dismounted to take the reins, the footman jumped down to let down the steps and hand the ladies out, and they went quickly into the shop where haberdashery and millinery in the centre divided the grocery side from the counters where bales of linen and silks were displayed.

Under the younger ladies' advice turquoise blue was selected for the Dowager and a length ordered to be sent to the Dower House, and she was only just prevented from ordering another length of crimson to be sent to Miss Cheriton, and persuaded to exchange it for a lavender grey as being more suitable for her sister. And then while Melissa, at Sarah's request, selected a silk for herself from the rainbow medley that Mr. Briggs produced, one bale after another, for her inspection, and because the shop was over full of farmers' wives and daughters, young Lady Tamporley walked to the door intending to wait for the others in the carriage. As she stepped on to the pavement outside however the wind met her so boisterously that she had to stop and hold on to her bonnet with both hands to prevent it being whisked from her head and blown over the church steeple. And as she won her battle with the wind and the bonnet she found a young man in a faded blue coat, whose threadbare seams were mercilessly revealed by the bright, clear sunshine, in conversation with her footman.

'The gentleman is asking where Mr. Taylor's warehouse is, please, m'lady,' explained the lad. 'And I've been trying to tell 'un, but being furrin' like I doubt if he'll understand, and he don't seem to cotton to my lingo neither.'

Sarah asked where the warehouse was and on being told that it was in River Lane, just off the market-place, she turned quickly to the young man, who at the sound of her voice had turned equally quickly, and with a flush of warm pleasure she recognised Miss Cheriton's Romantic Frenchman.

'Lieutenant Cadot!' she cried. 'We meet again.'

'But it is hard to avoid meeting one's friends in this little town, where even the cobble-stones are old acquaintances!'

'I hope that does not mean that you dislike them for it?' she said.

'On the contrary, England has been as kind to me as a captor can be to a captive, madame.' Between their thick black fringe of lashes his eyes were the colour of smoke. Certainly he was a most romantic figure. She said a little breathlessly:

'It is natural to be a little restless at this time of year.'

'When the buds swell,' he agreed in French, 'and the sun begins to warm the earth, and hope revives in men's hearts.'

She was about to say that the course the war was taking could not add much to such a hope where he was concerned when the Dowager came out of the shop to fetch her in to help Melissa in her choice of silks, and Sarah had to introduce him to her. She was amused to see the expression on the lady's face as the Frenchman bowed with a grace equal to that of the old Comte and swept her hand to his lips.

'I have heard about you, Monsieur Cadot,' said the Dowager frostily. 'From my sister, Miss Cheriton.'

'Oh yes, Mademoiselle Cheriton and I are old friends.' His voice was low and charming and the Dowager, whose heart was never as stony as she would have liked it to be, thought that her sister's raptures had not been so misplaced after all. This Mr. Cadot was certainly an extremely handsome young man, which added, unfortunately to the romance of his situation, and she thought it might be as well if Melissa took a little longer over her choice of silks. It was scarcely the time for her to be meeting a romantic young Frenchman, and after all her choice in making a selection of a new dress was not the same as her own or dear Sarah's. A Rector's daughter had to choose material and colour with her mind on her position in the parish, and also with some regard to the monthly balls of several years to come. She said with dignity, 'I am sorry that Tamporley is beyond the limit of your parole. I would have been pleased had you been permitted to visit me at the Dower House, Lieutenant.'

'Your ladyship is too kind.' But his eyes looked as if he were laughing, and her ladyship felt that at any moment her lips might betray her in an answering smile. She drew herself up.

'Sarah, my love, Melissa is finding it quite impossible to make up her mind over these silks. I must go back and tell her which one to have or we shall be here all day and Briggs will be driven out of his mind.'

'Very well, and I will tell Lieutenant Cadot what he wants to know.'

The Dowager left them and they looked at each other with the satisfaction that two children find in being unexpectedly let out of school. Sarah explained in her careful French where the warehouse was situated and that his nearest landmark to River Lane was the statue of King George in the market-place.

'A rotund gentleman on a horse,' she explained, her eyes demure. 'His Majesty visited Doverton once and dined with the Mayor and was so delighted with the dinner of boiled mutton and onions that he gave him that he presented the town with the horse trough that is beneath the statue, for the use of those poor horses who have to drag their laden farm carts up the hill to the market.'

'But the English are always so kind to their animals!' He was laughing again now, his expressive hands lending animation to the words. She noticed that he was carrying a box under his arm and admired its workmanship, asking if it had been made by the prisoners at the Castle.

'But yes.' He opened the box, which was a beautifully fashioned wooden one ornamented with elaborate marquetry, and he showed her a little ship made of finely carved bone inside it. 'The box and the ship were made by my servant, Lecointre, and his friend, Fouquet, and as this good merchant, M. Taylor, could not come to the prison market this week because he was suffering from the gout, I have undertaken to carry it to him.'

'And what will you do if Mr. Taylor is not at his warehouse?'

'I shall endeavour to find his private house – unless he should happen to live above his shop.'

The footman, to whom Sarah applied once more for information told them that Mr. Taylor's house was outside the town, on the far side of the Heath just before one came to the turnpike.

'Ah then, so long as it is on this side of the turnpike I shall be safe.' The Lieutenant smiled his relief. 'One cannot move a turnpike, Madame.'

Sarah met his eyes mischievously. 'Have you moved other boundaries then?'

'Not I, Lady Tamporley, but a friend of mine, Captain Desparde, moved a milestone once. He fell in love with the daughter of a farmer who used to visit our market. She was a pretty, buxom girl, with the round red cheeks and flaxen hair of so many of your English country girls. But to this Captain Desparde she was a goddess. Unfortunately her father's farm

3

lay a few metres beyond the milestone that marked the end of our parole, and so Desparde borrowed a wheelbarrow and a spade and he moved the milestone to the other side of the farm. But in moving it he injured his back and was taken into hospital, while M. Le Fermier packed his daughter off to an aunt in Yorkshire.'

'A sad story, but one with a moral, as my Mamma would say. One should be content with one's limitations, Monsieur!'

'But, Lady Tamporley, there are some circumstances in which I could find myself utterly content.'

She pretended that she did not understand, but her eyes told him to the contrary, and her heart felt lighter than it had done in years. 'I must go and help in this important choice of silks,' she murmured.

'You have made your choice, no doubt?'

'Oh yes, that was easy.'

'I can understand that.' He dropped his voice and still speaking in French added, 'White, shot with gold . . . or Madonna blue.'

She knew that she should be angry with him for his impudence but she was not: never had the sunshine been so bright, or a March day so lovely. She said goodbye softly and quickly and went back into the shop.

'You were a long time telling that man the way,' grumbled the Dowager. 'He was only pretending that he did not understand English, Sarah my love. He understood me perfectly when I spoke to him! All you have to do with foreigners is to speak loudly and clearly, and they know at once what you mean.'

'Tam must be very good with them then,' said Melissa, eyeing the many silks in front of her in despair.

'Oh yes, he never has any difficulty,' said the Dowager. 'Now Sarah, my love, please tell Melissa which of these silks she is to have without any more delay.'

'She is to have my rose-pink,' said Sarah smiling. 'Yes, Mel dearest, I insist. I could see that you liked it when I chose it and you did not like to say so. It will suit you perfectly. Mr. Briggs!' She raised her voice and poor little Mr. Briggs turned, almost losing his balance under the weight of yet another bale of silk, apple-green this time, that he had pulled down from an upper shelf. 'Please pack up the length of rose-pink for Miss Melissa and send it with Miss Cheriton's lavender grey. I have changed my mind. You may send me a length of that white one with the little gold pattern on it.'

'But m'lady, it is a fleur de lys!' cried Mr. Briggs, scandalised. Sarah laughed.

'Nobody will know what it is, and I am sure I do not mind. I shall invite our dear old émigré to dinner when I wear it for the first time and he will be delighted.' The ladies left the shop and Mr. Briggs called an assistant to stack the silks away again, and when they came out of the carriage the Romantic Frenchman had gone.

Only Sarah caught sight of him a little while later as the carriage made its way back to Doverton, standing reading the inscription on the base of the statue with a slightly pensive air.

'This statue,' he read, 'was raised by the people of Doverton in gratitude for His Majesty's beneficence in providing a water trough for the horses that attend the market . . . ' He chuckled as he read, and then he raised his eyes to the statue. A rotund gentleman indeed! 'These English,' he told himself wryly, 'they do not behead their monarchs – at least not in these days. They laugh at them instead.' He frowned, thinking that perhaps it was better so in the end. Nobody could have laughed at poor, unfortunate Louis XVI: he had been answerable to nobody but himself. The English King was responsible to Parliament for his actions, and English nobility had helped the Commons to rule for many generations, unlike the French noblemen who had no say in the government of their country. They were only required to be courtiers surrounding one man whose word was law, and therefore when he perished they had to perish too. But you could not explain these things to the English. They had not listened, as he had listened, to his uncle's friends as they sat round the lawyer's table in the modest house on the outskirts of Paris, talking of Napoleon, and how the whiplash of his astonishing personality had made one nation of their chaotic country, and drawn Frenchmen together in one army, pledged to fight the enemies of France.

With a shrug of his shoulders he dismissed Farmer George and his boiled mutton and his horse troughs from his mind and walked on down Market Street and past the dark, secretive little turning that led down to Madame Genie's house at the bottom. The house was discreetly veiled now in heavy curtains and the windows were close shut: only in the evenings and at night did it and its tenants awake.

He wondered what had taken Sir Tamporley Brevitt Tamporley to Madame's house on the day when they had met in the narrow hall-way.

'You're a Frenchie, aren't you?' Sir Tamporley had said in his arrogant way. 'Thought this sort of thing was out of bounds . . .'

'To the English officers at the Castle, Monsieur, not to the French,' Philippe had said smoothly.

The baronet stared at him suspiciously and seemed about to give him the lie when Madame had come and said something to him in a low voice and he had stamped away after her, up the steep stairs.

Lieutenant Cadot had wondered then at the appetite of the man and now he wondered still more. You would have thought he had all he needed in the little Madonna in his Great House at Tamporley. But the truth of it was of course that it was not in the nature of man to be satisfied. Give him a princess and he wanted a milkmaid: give him a milkmaid and he would cry for his lost princess. Ah well, maybe it was better to give dancing and French lessons to these English ladies and teach their menfolk how to fence, or to be like Lecointre and his friend Fouquet and make model ships out of the bones from the Castle cook-house. From the five years that he had spent in England he had learned to like the English, although some of their characteristics would continue to annoy him, and Englishmen like the large, boorish husband of little Lady Tamporley he found particularly irritating. For one thing they persisted in speaking to their wives as if they were situated in the middle of a field, or else had been born deaf, and from his own experience of English ladies he was quite sure that they were not deaf, and given a little encouragement they were not dumb either.

As for Sarah, on her way home in the carriage, she could only hear the low, caressing tones of Lieutenant Cadot's voice as he had told her that her dress should be white shot with gold or Madonna blue. The implication of the words could not be mistaken, and their meaning was flattering to a woman who had worn a cap since she was seventeen. She could not help seeing the expression on his handsome face, like that of little James when he wanted something, or Tam, in the old days when he had come courting her. And what a long time ago that seemed, on this sparkling day, and how easily he had developed into the shouting, ranting, pompous Tam of today. . . .

She sighed a little, forgetting how she had boasted of her contentment with her lot barely an hour or so ago, when Melissa had laughed at her and told her to take care, or the gods might be listening.

# 4

At ten o'clock that morning Lecointre had come up the rickety stairs that led to the French officers' quarters in the keep and placed the model ship in its fine box on Philippe Cadot's table.

'Voilà, my Lieutenant!' he said, standing back so that he could admire it. 'Regard then the *Redoutable* – as complete and as beautiful as the day when she sailed into her last battle against the English. Isn't it wonderful then what may be accomplished with a handful of bones?'

'And the skill of clever fingers too, Gaston.' Philippe glanced at the excitable little man affectionately. 'Your friend Fouquet is a true artist. But why build the *Redoutable*? Surely the *Victory* would have a better sale?'

'I said the same. I said to Fouquet, "My friend, we want to sell this ship. The *Victory* would fetch more than the poor old *Redoutable*".'

'And what did he say to that?'

Lecointre shrugged. 'He said there were too many *Victorys*. Every man that built a ship named it the *Victory*. But he said he was a Frenchman and proud of it, so he would make a French ship of the line and call it the *Redoutable*, which foundered in fighting the English at Trafalgar, and from whose decks came the shot that killed the great Admiral Nelson himself. It was his gesture of defiance, Fouquet said, to our captors.'

Philippe laughed. He had no liking for the sardonic Fouquet but he could hear his arrogant tones declaiming his sentiments as Lecointre spoke. 'It is certainly a gesture!' he agreed. 'Although, mind you, I think Fouquet may be right and that it may appeal to the English, who love to decry themselves at all times and give credit to their enemies. Such magnanimity is a form of their conceit!' He asked which part of the ship had been made by Gaston and was told that he had made none of it.

'I am far too clumsy for such delicate work, Lieutenant. I only find the materials, and when the bone is carved it is I who polish it. I too discover the wood for the box – a difficult business that, because the English peasants carve wood also for sale, and like the straw plaiting and the lacemaking which they filched from us, they are jealous in case we make much better wooden things than they do – which would not be hard to do, diable, because these peasants over here are clumsy and half-starved and take no trouble with their work. But the box is charming, is it not, with the light woods patterned into the dark, and the battle scene painted on the back of it behind the ship?'

'Fouquet is an artist, as I said before. But there is metal here too, and it looks like gold. Whose ear-rings did you steal for that?'

'Joseph Maugin's, but I did not steal them. I bought them from him and he held out for a big price, that one. I was forced to go to the Agent and ask for some of the money he holds for me, because what with buying the rings and paying the goldsmith's fee for melting them and working the metal for us, it cost me nearly five pounds.'

'But Fouquet shared the expense, surely?'

'That is a good joke!' Lecointre laughed. 'He never has a sou in his pocket, that one, though he has sold many of his beautiful carvings in the prison market. But he has not a penny lodged with Captain Buller.'

'But what does he do with it then?' Philippe caught the expression of the little man's eyes and understood. 'You have told me of this before I think. He is a gambler, this man Fouquet.'

Gaston spread his hands resignedly. 'My poor friend,' he commiserated. 'He loves these games of chance, whatever they may be – the choice of a card, the longest of three straws, the toss of a coin – it is all the same to him. He lives only for these wagers, and even his food goes to pay his debts.'

'But that is strictly forbidden. No prisoner is allowed to gamble away his clothes, his bedding or his rations. Fouquet knows that as well as you do.'

'But all Frenchmen will gamble, my Lieutenant, and you cannot stop these things. And then you see it is all he has. For you there is a walk in the town outside the Castle walls, there is conversation with the people in the streets and in the shops, there are houses open to you to visit, and beyond the town there are the green fields to look at, even if you may not go into them. There is in fact, except for this trifling matter of your word of honour, all the freedom in the world. For me too in the prison here there is conversation because I like to visit my friends and talk and do a hand's turn here and another there. I learn many trades, I fetch and carry at the hospital, and I do your work, Lieutenant. I light your fire, I forage for wood and coals for you, I brush your boots and your clothes. In short I am continually occupied. But for this poor Fouquet there is nothing except his carving and his painting, and when the daylight is gone he sits with others round a rushlight and wagers his soul away for amusement.'

'He should be an officer's servant, like you. It would lend variety to his life and even threepence a day would add to his wagers.'

'Fouquet will be no man's servant. He says he works only for himself and for France.'

'Such arrogance will be his downfall.'

'It will indeed, and so I tell him, but what can you do against this colossal obstinacy? Mon dieu, sometimes I tell him

40

that he must be the son of an aristocrat, to have such pride. It makes him furious, that. He is a true republican.'

'While you, of course, are for the Emperor?'

'But of course, Lieutenant.' Gaston's black eyes met Philippe's drolly and he laughed.

'You know quite well that if the Bourbons ever came back to France you'd wear the white cockade with the rest of us.'

'I am a Frenchman, my Lieutenant, and as long as I have food in my stomach and good health that is all I require of any man.'

'A philosopher, Gaston.'

'If you say so.'

Philippe left politics alone and went back to the ship.

'It is no good looking to me to buy it,' he said. He had only his ten shillings a week allowance, which had to be helped out by lessons in the town: he could not even afford the lodgings outside the prison as some of his brother officers could. But Gaston assured him that they already had a buyer for the ship, the merchant, M. Matthew Taylor, who had promised to buy her for thirty pounds.

'That is a good price,' agreed Philippe.

'It is for a year's work, Lieutenant.'

'Then it is not such a good price, although he could argue I suppose that you had your board and lodging free during the time you worked on her.'

Gaston then told him about the merchant's gout that had prevented him coming to the market that day, and how his apprentice had given him a message asking if one of the officers who were on parole could take it to his house, as the gentleman who was going to purchase it from him was to visit Doverton the following day. 'And so, my Lieutenant,' added Gaston hopefully, 'that is why I am here.'

'I see. I am to be your carrier?'

'If you please, Monsieur.'

'I will with pleasure, as long as M. Taylor's house is not out of bounds. I will not break parole again even for you, Gaston.

41

Five times I have broken it in the past month – it is true for only a few hours at a time – but the excellent Captain Buller says that if it happens again I will be confined to barracks, and that is no mean threat with the summer only a couple of months away!'

'At least Captain Buller is a kindly man. He will not be likely to send you to a prison ship, Lieutenant!'

'God forbid!' The Lieutenant had had experience of the hulks at Chatham, as Lecointre and Fouquet had at Portsmouth, and he had as little desire as they had to return to them. 'I will first of all visit this good merchant's warehouse in the town and find out where M. Taylor lives,' he said.

'But if M. Taylor is not there do not leave our ship with this villainous apprentice, Hicks,' warned Gaston. 'He will not let you have the money, and I do not trust that one. He has eyes like a pig.'

Philippe promised that he would give the ship to nobody but Mr. Taylor himself. Gaston then brushed his best blue coat, shabby as it was, and eased it over his shoulders, and polished the new boots that had recently been made in the town and paid for with the price of many French lessons. The Lieutenant's curly dark hair was brushed and his tall hat with its silver buckle placed at an angle on his head, the ship was tucked under his arm and his cane placed in his hand and he set off for the town, passing the sentries at the Castle gates without even being requested to show his pass because they know him so well. The handsome Frenchman was popular with everybody in the prison, with the possible exception of the turnkey at the gate that overlooked the cobbled street down into the town, but it was Philippe's experience that most turnkeys were soured by the years they had passed in looking after men in captivity.

'Damned Frenchies,' he growled looking after the Lieutenant. 'How they mince along, as if they was dancing instead of walking!'

As Philippe went down the street, however, he was not thinking so much how to place his feet as how to avoid the sharper cobblestones and any loose flints that might catch his toe. Although his beautiful new boots were well cut and sewn they were fashioned of a poor quality leather, which was all he had been able to afford, and he had to walk carefully if he were not to damage them.

The sunshine was gaining strength away from the wind and the street sloped steeply, the roofs and the curling smoke from the chimneys stepping down in front of him as he walked until it seemed to him, not for the first time, that it would have been quicker to walk from roof to roof and chimney to chimney.

But his feeling of well-being increased with every step. Gaston's remark about the prison ships had sent his thoughts back to the time when he was first captured, five years ago, when he had never dreamed he would enjoy the liberty he now had in England. Officers and men had been herded together, nine hundred of them in one stripped battleship of the line. They were given the same ill-fitting yellow uniforms to wear as Gaston and his friends had now, in case they tried to escape, the air in the cabins was foul, the food uneatable, and if dysentery or small-pox broke out among them they died like flies. This charming English town and even its grim old Castle that was their prison seemed a paradise when he was transferred there later.

And after his meeting with Sarah outside Mr. Brigg's shop that morning it seemed more charming to him still, and he continued on his way happily and found the large shop that Mr. Taylor honoured by the name of a warehouse, in River Lane, without much trouble.

Philippe found however that he distrusted Mr. Taylor's apprentice as much as Lecointre had done: Josiah was a tall lanky young man with a fawning manner, but his eyes were small and wicked, and his smile sly and false.

'Mr. Taylor is at his home with the gout,' he said when Philippe had stated his business. 'I told the Frenchy prisoner when he brought the ship to the market at nine this morning,

I said, "Look here, Frenchy, it is no good looking for Mr. Taylor here today, and you'd better let me have the ship now you've finished it. I'll take it to him and he'll pay you for it later." But this he refused to do, I dunno for why. Dian't trust me, I s'pose, insolent Frenchy dog. The word of an Englishman's better than a Frenchy's word, I'd say.'

'Would you indeed?' Lieutenant Cadot studied him thoughtfully and there was a glitter in his eyes. 'But what you have to say does not interest me, my friend. It is a fine day for walking and I know where Mr. Taylor's house is situated. I will take it to him myself this afternoon.'

'Take care you don't put a foot on the Heath as you go, then,' shouted Josiah after him as he left the shop. 'It's out of bounds remember, to the likes of you.'

The Lieutenant turned and smiled politely, thanking him for reminding him of the circumstance, and then he went back to the town and visited The Creaking Gate, an inn whose name was all that was left of what had been the Crighton Gate to the Castle in the old days. The bread and cheese there was excellent and the beer a great deal better than the poor thin stuff supplied to the prisoners at the Castle. It was a friendly house and a popular meeting place for Philippe and his friends, and occasionally he would be invited by one of his wealthier compatriots to join him in dinner there. The landlady's cooking was the best in the town, but she never held his poverty against him. She would serve him with his bread and cheese and stay and gossip as happily as if he had ordered roast goose or a pigeon pie.

She came to the table where he was showing a friend the little model that he was taking to the merchant that afternoon, and she exclaimed at its perfection, but when he went on to tell her where he was taking it she looked at him quickly and dropped her voice.

'See that you get back by nightfall then, sir,' she said. ' 'Specially if any money changes hands . . . That Heath can be a rare lonely place nights, and there's no moon just now.

44

There've been some nasty robberies up here of late – ay, and murders too.'

'A thousand thanks, Madame, but I shall be back at the Castle long before nightfall. Our winter curfew is still standing at five o'clock and will continue to do so for another month yet.'

'That is a good thing then.' She glanced at some of the other Frenchmen at the table. 'P'raps one of your friends will walk with you, sir?'

'Oh no. I shall walk briskly. I shall be well enough by myself.' And he finished his beer and the last of the cheese and started out.

Very soon the town was left behind and he was out on the road through the Heath, which was quiet and lovely, the only living creatures in sight beside himself being the sheep, cropping the turf ever shorter and gazing at him with mildly astonished eyes as he came up the road. Ahead of him he could already see Mr. Taylor's house in its belt of leafless trees and the dark laurels that made the shrubbery beneath them, and he slackened his pace, knowing that he had plenty of time.

The distance was deceptive however and the road flinty, and again he had to walk carefully if he wished to save his boot leather, so that it was already past three when he arrived.

He was admitted at once by a neat maid-servant to a room where her master was sitting, with his bandaged foot on a footrest. The merchant greeted him kindly, shaking his hand and telling him to sit down and rest himself, while the maid was sent off to fetch madeira wine and plum cake. He admired the little model whole-heartedly, saying that it was even better than he had hoped.

'There is no doubt that Fouquet is a clever devil,' he said, turning it so that the light from the window caught it. 'My customer will be delighted with it.'

Philippe glanced at the windows and seeing that the sun had only just started to move down behind the merchant's tall trees settled himself to enjoy the wine and Mr. Taylor's conversation. There was nothing he liked more than being made welcome in an English home, and he found Mr. Taylor ready to talk about France, which he had visited frequently before the Revolution, when his father was alive and he had been sent abroad to purchase silks and laces there. He knew Paris well and spoke regretfully of the large town mansions that had belonged to the aristocracy of France.

'The Faubourg St. Germain,' he said. 'There was a fine district for you, Monsoor. I'll wager there were some treasures in those houses – or 'otels, as they called them then – before the Revolution swept them all away!'

'But Monsieur, revolutions are like time: they have a habit of sweeping things away.'

'Sometimes that can be a good thing,' admitted the merchant, 'as long as they put something better in their place. But did France, Monsoor? Can you answer me that?'

'As to that,' said Philippe smiling, 'she put Napoleon Bonaparte there, and some of us have not thought that to be a bad thing.'

'Boney?' Mr. Taylor chuckled. 'What a man! I have heard that most of his success was due to the speed with which he moved during his campaigns.' He glanced at the young French officer sympathetically. 'I'm afraid at the moment he is not doing very well. I am sorry for your sake, Monsoor, if glad for our own.'

The Lieutenant shrugged. 'In a little while no doubt he will recover,' he said. 'And then I will be offering you my condolences, Monsieur!' They both laughed, and then with a glance at the grandfather clock in the corner Mr. Taylor remarked that it was nearly half-past four and his visitor must be thinking about returning to the Castle.

'Mustn't be over-staying that curfew of yours,' he said. He got out of his chair and hobbled to a cupboard beside the clock and unlocked it and counted out thirty pounds in Bank of England notes. 'They will not make such a bulge in your pocket,' he commented. 'Safer than carrying gold across the Heath.'

'I am not afraid,' said Philippe smiling. He tucked the money away in his breast pocket and buttoned his coat across it and promised that he would come again for more conversation about his beloved Paris. The light was going now, and the trees down the carriage-way were deep enough in shadow to conceal an army. As he came out on the road he realised that he had spent more time than he could afford already, and that if he were not willing to sacrifice his boots to the flints he would not get back to the Castle before the gates were shut against him.

He glanced about him quickly and then at the Heath: the path across it, cutting short his walk by a good few minutes, was still clearly defined and the road was empty. There did not appear to be a soul in sight ready to start a hunt after a French prisoner breaking his parole. He hesitated only a moment before crossing the road and leaving it for the turf, grateful for its aromatic scent as his feet crushed it, and glad of its springy softness for his ill-used boots.

The path led up over the crest of the Heath and then dropped down towards the stream that ran through it at the bottom, making its way from the Tamporley woods far away to the right to the bridge that spanned the Doverton road on the left. There were only stepping stones across the stream here, with a dark clump of fir trees that stood like sentinels beside them.

The dying rays of the setting sun fell across the path behind him as he reached the firs, and it was then that he saw a tall shadow move in the trees. He put his foot quickly on the first stone, but before he could spring from it to the next the man who had been waiting in the trees delivered a blow that sent him reeling down into the water, and then he stood over him and hit him again.

The Lieutenant's last thought before he went down into unconsciousness was, 'Mon dieu, now they'll send me back to one of those damned prison ships for sure . . .'

# 5

In the spring of the year Miss Cheriton went through her wardrobe and laid out on her bed those dresses that would bear repair and those that could be re-made with the help of new trimming and old lace. The same dressmaker who visited the Dowager and young Lady Tamporley came to examine the dresses, but it was seldom that any new lengths of material were waiting there to be examined and admired when she came to the little house in the High Street. The lavender grey silk required the most careful examination of the fashions, so that not one inch should be wasted, and every fold should show it forth to the best advantage.

On the morning after Melissa had visited Mr. Brigg's shop with the Dowager and Sarah, Miss Cheriton laid out the length of silk on her bed with complete disregard for the dresses in her wardrobe, and she was extremely glad when one of the Tamporley carriages arrived at the same time as the dressmaker with a note from Sarah asking Melissa to spend the day with her.

*We will see if the violets are out in the Tamporley woods,* she wrote. *And then we will call upon M. Estoban. He was asking after you, dearest Mel, when he dined with us.*

'Well, I daresay the Comte will have had his breakfast by the time you arrive,' said Miss Cheriton. 'That old Jeanne of his takes him his chocolate and rolls at twelve, I believe,' Jeanne was the old Breton woman who looked after the émigré in Tamporley village, and after she had served him with his *petit déjeuner* she would allow the village barber to visit him, to shave him and to powder his hair, and to help him into his coat.

M. le Comte d'Estoban found it impossible to alter the habits of a life-time, and for him the village barber in Tamporley, John Birney by name, had taken the place of his valet. If he had not come to shave him every morning and to tie his cravat and powder his hair he did not know what he would have done. It was as natural to the Comte to have Birney there as it was to have his shirt ruffles starched, and his hair powdered still. Flour was scarce in England, and the English went short of starch, even Sir Tamporley Brevitt Tamporley's shirt ruffles being limp, and for a long time now Englishmen had worn their hair short and unpowdered. But the Comte still had his fine handkerchiefs scented with lavender water, and his white hands, with their one great ring, did no more manual labour than taking up a pen now and then to write his memoirs – a work that had never progressed beyond a few pages in all the years that he had been in England.

Nobody would have thought in talking to him that he existed on a quarter of a tiny annual sum left him by an English relative of his wife's, three-quarters finding its way into the pockets of other émigrés who still lived, like himself in England, because for them, as for him, there was nobody and nothing left to tempt them to return to France.

In the past Melissa had enjoyed visiting the Comte. His courtliness, his gaiety and his witty conversation charmed her, while his compliments on her dress and her looks restored the self-confidence that her encounters with her cousin Tam tended to have shaken. She felt that Tam regarded the émigré in the light of a bad debt that he had inherited from his father, but Tam or no Tam she felt in need of compliments that morning, and was as delighted to accept Sarah's invita-

4

tion as her Aunt Charity was to have the new lavender silk and the dressmaker to herself.

So Melissa set off happily in the carriage on that March morning, her hands tucked into a fur muff against the keen North East wind that seemed to find its way through the closed carriage windows, and as she went she wished that Englishmen were as free with their compliments as M. Esteban. But the most that Englishmen of her acquaintance would say was that a dress or a ribbon was becoming to her, and that reluctantly, as if the admission had been dragged from them under protest and no attention should be paid to it.

Sarah was waiting for her in her little sitting-room upstairs and as they greeted each other with delight Melissa thought once more what a very pleasant place the park could be when Mrs. Forsett was away, and she hoped that poor Sophy's new admirer would take a long time in coming to the point.

The two girls set off together in the March sunshine, making their way towards the woods where the first violets grew, and as they walked they chattered about the children, and the Dowager, and their Aunt Charity, and the Comte, and Tam's new chestnut filly, and the children again, and even of Miss Pope, but they did not spoil the morning once by mentioning Mrs. Forsett's name.

A rustic bridge, with gates at each end, crossed the ha-ha ditch that separated the wood from the park, preventing the cattle that grazed there from killing themselves by eating indigestible trees, and as Sarah and Melissa crossed the bridge and walked down the path that skirted the trees and led to the bank where the violets grew, the force of the wind was broken by a cluster of young larches, pink-tasselled and gay.

The bank faced into the sun and they came upon it to find as they had anticipated that the violets were out, white and blue, carpeting the grassy bank. But it was not at the violets that they looked in that first moment, as they stopped and clutched each other, the colour draining from their faces because they were almost too horrified to scream.

Because there, in the midst of the violets, they saw Miss Cheriton's Romantic Frenchman, Lieutenant Philippe Cadot, sprawled face upwards on the bank, with his head and hair matted and stained with blood, and lying as motionless as if he were dead.

\*     \*     \*

The two girls forgot the violets and after a first gasp of horror they ran to him, and Sarah dropped on her knees beside him and felt his forehead. It was warm and he was still breathing, although his face was grey. She looked about her quickly and then remembering the stream that meandered through the bottom of the coppice she told Melissa to take her handkerchief and soak it with water and come back with it as quickly as she could. Melissa ran off with the handkerchief and was back in a few minutes and Sarah gently bathed his face.

After a little of this treatment he stirred and opened his eyes, staring at young Lady Tamporley blankly at first, and then with a smile of sudden if painful recognition.

'An angel from heaven,' he whispered and then he closed his eyes again and looked even worse than before.

'If Tam catches him here,' said Melissa grimly, 'it won't be as an angel from heaven, but a devil with horns and tail.'

'What are we to do?' cried Sarah softly, her voice shaking. 'Oh Mel! Can't you think of something?'

'I'll soak the handkerchief again,' said Melissa, 'and then I'll see if I can find somebody to help us with him. We are much nearer the road than the house down here, and there may be a villager passing by whom I could send, or bring back with me.' She was soon back again with the freshly soaked handkerchief and ran off down the path that led towards the road to the village, while Sarah applied the handkerchief a second time with rather more water, so that the Lieutenant's eyes opened again more quickly than before, and stared up into her eyes with a gleam that held a hint of laughter.

'Hold there, Lady Tamporley!' he protested weakly. 'I am not dead! You have recovered me, but not in order to be drowned.'

She gave a little sigh of relief. 'What happened to you?' she asked in distress. 'Did you have an accident?'

He told her what he remembered about the attack that had been made upon him the evening before. 'It is not for myself that I am distressed,' he added. 'I have a hard skull, and I don't suppose it is badly cracked, but it is those two poor prisoners at the Castle, who spent a year or more building the little ship that I sold for them to Monsieur Taylor. I have been robbed of their earnings, and they will be expecting me back with the money. It is even possible that they may imagine I have made off with it myself.

'I am sure they will think nothing of the sort.' She had been gently bathing some of the blood away while he was talking. 'And you have come a long way from the Heath.'

'Is this not the Heath then?' He frowned and raised his head to look about him and then dropped back with a groan. 'Where am I?'

'In the park at Tamporley.'

'Tamporley? Mon dieu, that is out of bounds indeed! But how did I get as far as this?'

'Do you not remember?'

'I seem to recollect picking myself out of the stream where the fellow had left me – no doubt hoping I would drown – and then trying to follow the stream to the road back to Doverton. But it was very dark by that time and I must have wandered off in the opposite direction.'

'Yes, we are more than a couple of miles from the Doverton road. This is the opposite side from the Castle.'

'That settles it!' He made a wry face. 'Captain Buller will not be able to swallow this. It will be the hulks for me!'

He smiled at her worried expression. 'In the meantime it is no use to delay matters any more. I will get to my feet and make my way back to the road.'

'No, you are to stay where you are!' Her hand gently stopped him from making the attempt. 'My cousin has gone for help, and she will be back directly. In the meantime, Monsieur, stay still.' She moved a little nearer to him, and ever after that morning the bitter-sweet scent of young bracken thrusting up from the turf and freshly crushed by her movement brought back that moment. 'Supposing I were to take your head on my knee?' she said. 'It will be more comfortable for you while we wait.'

'It will spoil your dress,' he said weakly.

'I have plenty more.' She eased his head and shoulders on to her lap and he did not stop her.

'White shot with gold,' he murmured. 'Or Madonna blue...'

'All colours of the rainbow,' she said and her voice trembled a little and lilted a little and was more joyous than it had been for a very long time.

'Of course ... Rainbows reach up to Heaven, do they not? That is undoubtedly the way you descend to earth ...'

'Monsieur, you are talking nonsense ...'

'It is the wound in my head, Lady Tamporley. You must bear with me. I am made delirious by it ...' But the smoke-blue eyes were watching her intently and she was glad to see Melissa returning with a gentleman striding along beside her. Delirious or not, Miss Cheriton's Romantic Frenchman was quite the most disturbing young man that Sarah had ever met.

\*     \*     \*

When Melissa reached the road to her delight she saw a private carriage driven by postboys approaching her at a rapid pace, evidently bound for the Doverton road. She stepped out boldly in the path of the horses and signalled to their riders to stop, which they did with some unwillingness while the owner of the carriage put down the window and thrust out his head to see what the matter could be.

His expression changed abruptly as he saw Melissa, and a moment later, as recognition came to her too, if it had not been for the plight of the poor Frenchman she would have turned tail and fled.

'Miss Melissa Prestwick!' Edward Beaumont threw open the carriage door, leapt down into the road and walked quickly towards her. 'What on earth are you doing here? And what has happened? You look quite white . . Are you hurt? Or ill?'

'No . . . that is, *I* am not hurt, thank you.' She made a strenuous effort after composure and her confusion became worse than ever. She stared at him helplessly and wondered how she could ever have laughed at him. Surely the clear honesty of his grey eyes was infinitely better than the melting glances of a Frenchman, however romantic he might be! 'My cousin, Lady Tamporley, and I were looking for violets up there in the woods,' she went on in a hurry, 'and we came upon this poor Frenchman . . . one of the officers from the Castle prison. He has a terrible wound in his head and we don't know what to do.'

'I should not distress yourself. He has probably been fighting a duel,' said Mr. Beaumont coolly. 'I have heard that they do this sort of thing with deplorable frequency, no doubt caused by boredom.'

'But it is the back and side of his head!' protested Melissa. 'And he really does look very bad indeed.'

Mr. Beaumont said that he would come and see the man for himself. He told his servant and the postboys to wait and he set out beside Melissa for the path that led back to the violet bank. As she hurried along he kept pace with her at a more leisurely pace and said, 'You have not told me yet how you come to be staying at Tamporley?'

'I am staying with my aunt in Doverton,' she explained. 'And today, my cousin's wife asked me to spend the day with her. We had just reached the woods over there when we found poor Lieutenant Cadot, lying there unconscious.'

He glanced at her curiously. 'You know him then?'

'Oh yes. He is very well known and liked in Doverton.'

'I see.' Again his eyes came round to her embarrassed face with a hint of amusement. 'I have heard about these French officers,' he remarked drily. 'They are reputed to be possessed of considerable charm.'

Melissa was in no mood to discuss the charms of Lieutenant Cadot and his friends. All she wanted was to get help for him as quickly as possible, and she bitterly regretted not going up to the house for it instead of trying the road. Edward Beaumont had subtly changed since she last saw him: his manner indicated that he was secretly amused at her concern for the Lieutenant. Probably, she thought indignantly, he put it down to an attack of feminine vapours at the sight of a little blood.

She felt slightly triumphant when they reached the wood and Mr. Beaumont saw the Lieutenant for himself, with his injured head resting in Sarah's lap. His amusement left him abruptly and he hurried across the short space of turf between them and dropped on one knee beside the young man, glancing at his injured head in concern.

'This may be serious,' he said to Sarah in a low voice. 'How did he come by it?'

She told him all she knew and as she finished Philippe opened his eyes again, and seeing another man there a look of relief appeared on his handsome face.

'Ah Monsieur!' he cried. 'These ladies have been so good, but if you can get me on to my feet again I think I can reach the road now and trouble them no more . . .'

'You will stay where you are for the moment, sir,' said Edward Beaumont quickly. 'I think a surgeon should see this wound as soon as possible.'

'There is a surgeon at the prison.' Philippe spoke carelessly. 'He will kill me no quicker than any other.' His eyes met Beaumont's and a smile flickered between the two men, and Edward Beaumont found that he liked this injured Frenchman. He looked about him in some perplexity.

'My carriage is down there in the road,' he said. 'I will gladly take you back to the prison in it, sir. But this bleeding should be checked first.' He gave a sudden exclamation. 'I have it! We passed a cottage a few yards back on the road. I might be able to get you as far as that and beg water and a strip of clean linen to bind your head up before we go on.'

'A cottage?' said Melissa.

'He means the Comte's house,' explained Sarah. 'That is an excellent plan, Mr. . . . .'

'Beaumont,' he said.

'Mr. Beaumont. I am sure M. Estoban would help us. He is a dear old man and a great friend of mine.'

'But surely he is an émigré?' protested Philippe. 'I have heard about this old Comte, Lady Tamporley, and I don't think he would welcome me. I am an officer in the Emperor's army after all.'

'We cannot pay attention to things like that just now.' Edward Beaumont brushed his protests aside. 'You are injured, and all we want of this old gentleman is a little human kindness and I don't suppose he will deny you that. But do you think you can walk as far if I were to support you? It is not a long way to the cottage. You can see the chimneys through the trees beyond the stream.'

Lieutenant Cadot sat up and measured the distance to the chimneys, conscious of his throbbing head and a strong inclination to faint again. He said that he would do his best, and with a gallant gesture he struggled to his feet and would have immediately fallen if Mr. Beaumont had not caught him.

'Put your arm round my shoulders,' the latter said quietly 'I will take your wrist, so . . . then my other arm goes round

56

your waist . . . so! And there is really little need for you to walk at all. I can get you down to that cottage quite easily thus.'

'You Englishmen are so strong,' said Philippe, smiling pallidly. 'It is all this good rosbif, n'est-ce pas, Monsieur?'

'Undoubtedly it is the roast beef,' agreed Mr. Beaumont. 'You think about that, sir, while I concentrate on the ruts in the path, and we'll be at Monsieur le Comte's house in a very little while.'

Melissa ran on ahead, followed by Sarah, in order to warn Jeanne in advance, and they erupted into the peace of the Comte's little garden, where the old Breton woman had been washing out some of her master's shirts and was hanging them out to dry in the sun.

She turned her head on hearing the click of the latch to the little gate and as she saw the two girls and Mr. Beaumont and his charge behind them, she gave a little scream, while the shirts went down into the dirt.

'Miladi! . . . Mademoiselle Melissa!' she cried. 'What are you doing then? And who is that man?'

'A French officer, out on parole,' explained Melissa hastily. 'He was attacked and robbed last night, and Lady Tamporley told Mr. Beaumont that she knew M. le Comte would help him if he brought him here.'

'And what made miladi so sure of this, if you please?' Jeanne drew herself up as far as her short stature would permit, placed her hands on her broad hips and stared inimically from Melissa to Sarah and then to the two men behind them, her black eyes snapping with indignation as Mr. Beaumont calmly brought Philippe to the bench where she sat to prepare her vegetable for cooking and let him slip down on it. 'This officer, as you well know, miladi, is from the Castle prison. Very well, let him go back there! We have nothing to do with these officers of Bonaparte's army.'

Mr. Beaumont's eyes met Philippe's anxiously, and saw in them a quiet, if exhausted amusement. 'What is the old woman saying?' he murmured. 'Don't speak the lingo myself, but it seems to me that she is not giving you a welcome, sir.'

'She is *not* friendly,' agreed Philippe. 'But it is to be expected. I find that I am more exhausted than I thought, though, and if you will be so kind as to send somebody to the Castle for a cart to get me back there I will be eternally grateful. The old woman will not attack me, I think, and I will harm nobody by sitting on this bench until the militia arrives.'

'Damned if I'll do that.' Edward stared at the tight-lipped Jeanne and then appealed to Melissa. 'Can't you make her understand what has happened, Miss Melissa? He's her countryman after all, whether he's Boney's man or not.'

'I will speak to her,' said Sarah. She turned to the old servant and said with dignity, 'Jeanne, I am surprised at your attitude. This man is badly injured. Look at the wound in his head. You can see for yourself that it is bleeding still . . .'

'But he has a head on his shoulders, hasn't he?' Jeanne's voice became shrill. 'There were others, better than he is and bigger than that pig Bonaparte, who lost theirs don't forget, twenty years ago. We do not overlook that, M. le Comte and me. I will show this fine French officer the door, miladi, and this kind Englishman can drive him back to his prison, and if he dies on the way so much the worse for him, and so much the better for us. Ma foi, I will not insult the memory of M. le Comte's family, who perished at the hands of men like this, by even offering to wash the blood from his face.'

'Jeanne! My dear Jeanne, what has come over you? What are you saying?' The Comte d'Estoban suddenly appeared in the little garden, and while Edward Beaumont bowed awkwardly as Sarah introduced him Philippe Cadot turned his throbbing head to regard him with curiosity. He did not remember ever having seen a French aristocrat of the *ancien règime* before, and if he had felt less exhausted it would have been an interesting experience.

The Comte was small and spare, his face with its finely

58

cut features was the colour of old ivory, and his dark eyes were smiling and inscrutable. His clothes were as old-fashioned as his freshly curled and powdered hair, but they were of a fine material, and Philippe noticed the starched ruffles of his shirt and the lace-edged handkerchief between his white fingers. For his part the Comte's glance swept over the Lieutenant without any interest beyond politeness, and it was to Lady Tamporley and Melissa that he addressed himself after his protest to Jeanne.

'Lady Tamporley, I am enchanted to see you! Mademoiselle Melissa, your servant! I was told last night that you had arrived and have been impatiently waiting this moment.' He kissed their hands with a gallant bow and flourish of the lace handkerchief. It was like a play from a lost century, the Lieutenant thought wonderingly, to see him posturing there and waving his scented handkerchief. He glanced up at the tall Englishman to see how he was taking it, but Mr. Beaumont's face was quite expressionless as he waited for the acting to cease.

'M. Estoban, we have to beg your pardon!' Sarah's gentle voice broke the silence. 'I am afraid that in our concern for poor M. Cadot we forgot things that we should have remembered and your servant did right to bring them to our notice. Lieutenant Cadot is a French officer, Monsieur, and he was attacked and robbed on his way back to the prison last evening. You can see for yourself that he is injured, but if you will permit Mr. Beaumont to leave him here on this bench for a time, my cousin and I will walk back to the house and fetch some of the Tamporley servants and a carriage to take him back to the Castle. In that way we need detain Mr. Beaumont no further: he has already delayed his journey, I'm afraid, to assist us.'

The old man stood very still while she was speaking, and when she had done he lifted his hand in a small gesture for silence, while he turned to study his unwelcome visitor, observing coolly the wound in his head, his pallor, and the spirit with which he was trying to meet the situation. To him he said, speaking in his beautiful, cultured French, 'Is there a hospital at the prison, Monsieur?'

'Why yes, M. le Comte.'

'They will look after you there as they should?'

'They will look after me very well, I thank you.' Philippe's voice was as cool and impersonal as the older man's.

'But you do not wish to return there perhaps?' The dark eyes were unexpectedly keen.

'On the contrary, it is imperative that I should return as soon as possible.'

'But Monsieur!' In desperation Sarah appealed to Mr. Beaumont, telling him what had been said, and he frowned.

'I told you, sir,' he told Philippe quickly, 'I would bring you here to have your wound dressed, and I mean to see that it is done before I leave you. You cannot go to the Castle with it bleeding like that, you have already lost far too much blood. If this old woman refuses to find a piece of clean linen for you and a bowl of water, I'm damned if I won't get my man to unpack one of my boxes out in the carriage there and find a clean shirt to tear up. . . .'

'Monsieur is too good.' Philippe's eyes met his bafflingly. 'I am afraid however that my wits were in no state to take in the full implications of the situation. I shall return to the prison without dying on the way, and the hospital will receive my wound with sufficient excitement no doubt to prevent the good Agent from sending me to the Black Hole. But that matters not at all. What does matter is that I shall be able to tell my two friends there what has become of their money and to ask Captain Buller to repay them out of the money he holds for me. I cannot rest until that is done.'

'This no doubt can be arranged.' The Comte, speaking in English now, cut in on the conversation. 'From what part of France do you come, Lieutenant?'

'From Paris, Monsieur.'

'And your name?'

'Philippe Cadot.'

'And your father?'

'Is a notary there . . . I call him my father but he is really my uncle. I am his adopted son.'

The Comte considered him from what seemed to be an immeasurable distance for some minutes, and then he turned on the scowling Jeanne.

'Heat up some water and fetch clean towels and bathe this gentleman's head,' he directed. 'And then bind it with strips of linen.'

'Gentleman!' she cried contemptuously. 'What gentleman, then? I see none, only the bourgeois son of a notary in Paris, and you do not call *him* a gentleman I hope, M. le Comte?'

'Tiens!' He cut her short. 'Do as I say. And when you have done that, fetch food for him.' He addressed himself more courteously to Mr. Beaumont. 'This is how I will arrange the matter, Monsieur. I will trouble you again, if you will permit me, before you depart, to help this young man to a small unoccupied bedroom in my house.'

Here again Jeanne interrupted shrilly.

'Unoccupied, ma foi!' she cried. 'And for whom? For this rubbish? . . . All these years have we kept that room unoccupied for one person, and for one person alone . . . and this is what happens. A fine thing indeed! I suppose I am to fetch one of M. le Comte's nightshirts for this *gentleman* to wear?'

'Certainly.' The Comte cut across her grumbling crisply. 'And then you may wash his own shirt because it looks to me as if it needs a wash . . . Now, Monsieur Beaumont, if we may have your assistance . . . '

'I am at your disposal, sir.' Edward Beaumont assured him that he was in no hurry to continue his journey. 'I am only going as far as Dove Tye Hall to stay with friends there,' he added, and he lifted Philippe easily from the bench and helped him into the house, and up the steep stairs to the unoccupied room. It was a small room but scrupulously neat and the narrow bed was supplied with clean sheets and blankets as if the person for whom it was kept might arrive at any moment.

Edward Beaumont helped the Lieutenant to extend himself thankfully on the narrow bed, and having seen him arranged there the Comte stayed a moment to say that he would visit Captain Buller himself during the afternoon.

'I know the Agent well,' he said. 'To him I will explain everything and I will ask for an extension of your parole, Lieutenant Cadot, so that you may stay in my house until you are recovered. I will also ask that your two fellow prisoners may be given the money that you fancy you owe them.'

'M. le Comte is too kind.' Philippe tried to smile but the pain in his head turned it into a grimace instead. 'I cannot possibly repay you, Monsieur ... '

'I did not know that we were discussing payment.' M. Estoban became once more aloof and icy. 'Your servant, Monsieur. Your servant, Monsieur Beaumont!' He left them and descended the cottage stairs with the air of one who descended the staircase at Versailles, and left to themselves the two young men exchanged smiles, the Lieutenant casting up his eyes expressively.

'I have come across some of these French émigrés in London,' said Beaumont consolingly, in a low voice. 'Believe me, they are all as proud as Lucifer and prickly as thistles. You will have to choose your words with the old man.'

'That I can well understand, Monsieur. If I am not to be poisoned or have my throat cut by the old woman, I may well be frozen to death by her master. But unless I wish to appear as churlish as the one and as arrogant as the other I do not see how I can refuse this hospitality.'

'I will come and visit you as often as my host's arrangements permit,' said Mr. Beaumont comfortingly.

'And if they should not be arranging my funeral when you arrive I do not deny that I shall be delighted to have your company, Monsieur!'

'The name is Beaumont, sir ... Edward to my friends!'

'And to my friends I also am Philippe, Monsieur!'

They shook hands gravely. 'O revooer then, Philippe,' said

Mr. Beaumont with a great effort of memory from his school-days.

'To our next meeting, Edouard,' responded Mr. Cadot. And so they parted.

Mr. Beaumont went back to his carriage without seeing the ladies again as they had already left for the park.

'Melissa,' Sarah said as they went, 'did you hear what Mr. Beaumont said to M. le Comte? He is on his way to Dove Tye Hall . . . That is where the Halsteads live, Mel!' She gave her cousin's arm a shake. 'Mel, are you *listening*? I believe Mr. Beaumont may be the man who is poor Sophy's admirer . . . Mel, do you hear what I am saying to you?'

'Yes,' said Melissa.

'And don't you think I am right?' asked Sarah smiling.

'I think it is highly probable that you are right,' Melissa said, and there was a hollow sound in her voice.

# 6

That afternoon the Comte, true to his promise, ordered the chaise from the livery stables behind the Tamporley Arms in the village, and set out for the Castle and Captain Buller. The Comte had hired the same little chaise and the same fat grey pony for so long now that he looked upon both as his own property, an opinion that was shared by the owner of the livery stables, Sam Daws, whose daughter Patty was maidservant to Miss Cheriton in Doverton.

'Get the Count's chaise ready, Ted,' he would shout at the stable boy when the note in M. Estoban's pointed, beautiful handwriting arrived, and if at any time he had to hire it out to somebody else he would make an honour of it of which his customer could not but be aware. 'I haven't got a carriage in today,' he would say doubtfully, 'but I daresay you *might* be able to borrow the Count's little chaise if his lordship should happen not to be using it.' And Ted would be sent flying off up the street to the Comte's little house to ask if the chaise might be hired out for an hour or two. But only the most careful drivers were allowed to drive the pony, and the hours were jealously counted until he and the chaise were safely back in the stables again.

It was much the same throughout Tamporley village, because the villagers took their attitude towards their émigré from the Dowager Lady Tamporley and her gentle little daughter-in-law. The best of the produce and the brownest of eggs and the creamiest milk and butter from the Great

House were sent down to the Comte every day, while the choicest fruit and vegetables in the gardens at Tamporley also found their way to his table.

And the villagers did a little in their way to make the old man and his servant feel at home: the children would curtsey and doff their caps at his approach, the women at the cottage doors bobbed and smiled, the village blacksmith pulled his forelock in a respectful greeting. Posies of flowers too were left at his door, and rosy apples. 'Not so fine as the Great House apples for sure, sir, but her ladyship did say once she never tasted sweeter ones . . . ' For the Comte they felt nothing but friendliness although he did belong to the nation with whom their country had waged war for so many endless years. They saved their enmity for the French prisoners up at the Castle, who, if those who used their eyes were to be believed, had everything of the best and lived off the fat of the land, while the English who paid for it all could starve.

As the Comte went down the village street in his little chaise that afternoon his journey was as usual in the nature of a royal progress. It would not have hurt his pride either to have heard the comments of the villagers as he went by. 'Eh, the poor old gentleman looks rarely peaky this afternoon. He's beginning to fail, likely. If all Frenchies were like that 'un we wouldn't be at war with 'em, that's for sure.'

The Agent's house was outside the Castle walls, a pleasant square house, built eight years previously and surrounded by a garden. Like most of the Agents in charge of the prisoner of war camps Captain Buller had been in the Royal Navy, and a faintly nautical air was lent to the house by the flag-staff on the lawn in front, and the Union Jack that fluttered from it from sun-rise until sun-down each day. Except for the military guard at his doors one might have taken it for the house of a country gentleman.

Behind it however there rose the high surrounding walls of the Castle, fifteen to forty feet high in places, and six to ten feet thick. The ancient moat had been filled with water again and inside the walls the Castle grounds were divided into two sections by wooden stockades and a road that ran between them from the North Gate to the South. In one section was the keep, and in one of its towers the French officers were lodged on the first floor with store-keepers above, because the storehouses, offices and hospital were all on that side of the Castle. In the other section there were about twelve hundred prisoners, soldiers and sailors, housed in wooden, two-storied buildings, built with no chimneys because there were no fireplaces. It had been thought by the authorities when the place was taken over for a prison camp, that many prisoners, packed in tightly enough, would keep each other warm without the unnecessary expense of fuel for fires. At the North and South Gates of the Castle sentries were posted beyond the turnkeys' lodges inside and out.

Some yellow-uniformed prisoners were working in Captain Buller's garden under the eyes of the militiamen when the Comte arrived. They were talking and joking among themselves and seemed cheerful enough on that bright March day and the old émigré was pleased to see it. There were so many of his countrymen in England, as Wellington's victories sent them back from the Continent by the thousand.

At Doverton Castle there was usually a cheerful air among the prisoners though, and the Comte thought this was because they had a good agent in Captain Buller. The agent to a prison made all the difference to its inmates.

He was ushered into the Captain's office by one of the militiamen while another took the pony's head, and the Agent turned from a session with his head store-keeper to greet him.

'M. le Comte d'Estoban!' he said smiling. 'This is a pleasure.' He dismissed his store-keeper with the words, 'That is all then, Hobbs. I will make a note of these things. It is abominable that we have no allowance for such a necessary article as soap, and I will certainly order more candles and coals before next winter.' He conducted the Comte into the private parlour behind the offices, and offered him refreshment which the old gentleman refused.

'Well then, at least will you not sit down and tell me what I can do for you?' said the Captain. 'It is a long time since we met – in fact, I don't think I have seen you since the day when you told me you were going to London to attend the Queen's birthday ball at Carlton House. I think you said then that all the émigrés in England had been invited?'

'And our King as well,' said the Comte smiling urbanely. 'It was a very grand affair, Captain Buller. I could only wish that our clothes had matched the occasion, but I am afraid we were deplorably shabby to be received by the First Gentleman in Europe.'

'But there are some who have no opinion of the Regent's taste in clothes, Monsieur! He is over-fond of blue satin and embroidered waistcoats, so they tell me, and corpulence does not lend itself to the part of the fairy prince.' The Agent's voice was dry and then it warmed once more to the émigré. 'But I thought you must have gone back to France, as so many of your friends are doing.'

'Not many yet, Captain Buller. Monsieur has gone . . .'

'Monsieur? Oh, you mean your King's brother . . .'

'Exactly. And I have not heard that he was received with enthusiasm by the French people, in fact from all accounts the Allies have treated him with a most humiliating indifference. So, until the Allies – and the French – make up their minds that they want the Bourbons back I intend to stay where I am.'

'And I am very glad to hear it,' said the Captain and waited to hear more.

'You have a prisoner here, an officer by the name of Lieutenant Philippe Cador, I believe?' said the Comte.

'Indeed yes.' The Agent frowned. 'And I may as well tell you at once, sir, that I do not know what to do with that young fellow. He is a charming young man, with a most engaging manner, but he does not seem to know the meaning of honour.'

'That, Captain Buller, should not surprise you, surely? The

new generation of Frenchmen, bred of the Revolution, can scarcely have any knowledge of such an out-dated commodity.'

'Five times in a month he has over-stayed his parole,' grumbled the Captain. 'And this makes the sixth . . He does not come back until after curfew and sometimes not until the next day. Oh, he comes back in the end, mind you, and his explanations are always very plausible, although one can see that he does not expect one to believe in them . . . He was engaged in conversation and did not notice how the time was going . . . or it was raining and he was wearing his best coat and he would have been soaked to the skin had he not waited, but unfortunately the rain continued all night. The excuses come out so glibly that one suspects that shelter was taken in the house of a certain well-known lady in the town, and that the lady herself has more to do with the Lieutenant's absences than she should . . . But this time it is too much. I shall have to make an example of him.'

'I shall be sorry if you do, all the same, Captain Buller,' said M. Estoban smiling, 'because he is at this moment at my house with a broken head.' He related the story of the Lieutenant's unhappy encounter on the Heath, and added that he had asked for the two men, Lecointre and Fouquet, to be paid the thirty pounds that had been stolen from him out of his own account.

'But do you have as much money in the Lieutenant's account?' he added curiously.

'Oh yes, I hold more than that for him, although his man Lecointre has far more than he has. But then Lecointre is an industrious little rascal and makes a penny there and a penny here wherever he can. It would not hurt Fouquet to wait for his money though. He is an idle, good-for-nothing fellow and it is strange that he and Gaston Lecointre are such good friends.' He glanced anxiously at the Comte, concerned for the Lieutenant. 'How bad is the wound?'

'It is deep and has bled freely. I do not think the bone is cracked, but if I have your permission to keep him with me I

68

will call at the apthecary's house on my way home and tell him to call on me as soon as possible.'

Captain Buller studied him thoughtfully. 'There is the hospital here,' he pointed out. 'But once Cadot is moved in there he is out of the jurisdiction of the Transport Office and comes under the Sick and Hurt instead. He may have good food and he may have only thin gruel. Nobody can tell. And as the nurses are all taken from the prisoners here the nursing he has will not be skilled and may be highly incompetent and rough. Then we have lost our resident surgeon recently, and the authorities do not seem to be in a hurry to have him replaced while only last week we had another five hundred prisoners sent us, and we can take no more. There are a few surgeons among the prisoners of course, and they do their best, but officially we only have the surgeon from the town. Young Richard Maple who thinks far more of his horse-flesh than he does of his patients, and whose remedy for all ills appears to be blooding. I cannot think that such treatment will be very good for Cadot at the moment.'

'One would not think so certainly.'

'Young Maple expects to see all the sick in the hospital, so the superintendent tells me, in a scanty hour or two every evening, and I am afraid of an epidemic breaking out in the prison. The resident surgeon used to hold a roll-call every morning and any man who did not feel well, even if it were only a trifling matter like an inflamed throat or a rash breaking out on him, was examined by him at once in case it might be the onset of an incipient disease, which, once started in the crowded conditions that we have here, would spread like wildfire.' He paused. 'I have no doubt that the Lieutenant would be much better nursed by your old servant.'

'So I have your consent to keep him?' M. Estoban was gravely pleased. 'I shall have pleasure in telling him that. But there is another thing before I go – this payment of what he takes to be his debt to these two prisoners, his servant and the other man that you do not like.'

'I will send for them at once, and you shall discharge the Lieutenant's debt to them yourself, M. le Comte, although I maintain that it is no debt of his.'

The Agent went into his office and removed the sum of thirty pounds from the safe there, making the money into bundles of fifteen pounds each and entering it carefully in the debit column under Philippe's name in his book

Then he went back to the Comte in the parlour, and while they waited for the men to appear they talked of the bad winter and the drifts of snow that had cut Doverton off from the outside world, and the gales round the coast that had been some of the worst in living memory, and the March winds that had succeeded them, and the promise of a dry summer, because those weather prophets, the rooks, were building high in the Tamporley elms. And they said nothing at all about the news in the morning's paper, which gave an account of Wellington's victories in Europe that were threatening to sweep Bonaparte out of France.

\*   \*   \*

'I told you how it would be,' said Gaston Lecointre as he and his friend followed the soldier who had been sent to fetch them. ' "Lieutenant Cadot," I said, "is not the man to rob his friends. Depend on it," I said, "something has happened to him and as soon as he is able to send a message we shall hear from him".'

'Oh yes, and I can tell you what that message will be,' sneered Fouquet. ' "Lieutenant Cadot sends his regrets but he is now on his way to France and begs us to convey his compliments to all his friends at the Castle." I never expected anything else since you insisted on placing our ship in his hands. It was an insane thing to do.'

'But the Lieutenant had plenty of money with the Agent, my friend.'

'And if he goes to the Agent to draw out a sum of thirty

70

pounds he must explain what he wants it for,' Fouquet reminded him cryptically. 'Whereas he did not have to explain our money to anybody, did he? Such a sum as that would pay his coach fare to the coast and a passage on a smuggler's boat to France, and still give him twenty pounds in his pocket. Do you suppose if I had had a similar chance I would not have taken it?'

Gaston knew better than to argue when Fouquet was in this mood and he said no more until they were in the Agent's office, and there the presence of the émigré struck them both dumb. They stared at him in silence and waited for the Captain to speak.

'We must wait for an interpreter,' said Captain Buller. 'These men do not understand English very well.'

'Then permit me to be that interpreter, Captain Buller,' suggested the Comte courteously. 'What is it that you wish to say to them?'

'I want them to confirm that they are the men who made the ship in question,' said the Captain. M. Estoban translated the request and Lecointre answered him eagerly:

'But yes, M'sieu. Mistaire Taylor was indisposed with the gout and Lieutenant Cador said he would take our ship to him at his house and fetch our money. Thirty pounds, M'sieu.'

The Captain then asked the Comte to tell the men what had happened and he did so, but while he was speaking to Gaston his eyes went more frequently to Fouquet and he thought he had seldom seen in England a face that expressed so much ruthlessness and unreasonable cruelty. It was the face of a man who would not hesitate to drag men and women off to their deaths, and laugh as he did so, just as those other revolutionaries had done twenty years ago, spurred on by the dregs of the nation, the sans culottes, the barbarians from Marseilles . . .

Suppressing his emotions he told them drily and in as few words as possible how Philippe had been set upon and robbed

71

of their money, and he thought that their reception of the news was illuminating.

'Mon dieu!' Gaston cried, horrified. 'The good Lieutenant was not killed, surely, and all because of our little snip? This is terrible indeed . . . '

But Fouquet only growled out, 'Sacré, so our money is gone! The imbecile has lost it for us . . . A year's work gone for nothing. This is a fine story indeed, if one can believe it!'

Expressionless now and icy the Comte said that Cadot wished them to be paid out of the money that the Agent held for him, and here again the replies of the two men were in character, Lecointre declaring that he would not touch it, that the loss was a misfortune that might happen to anybody, and that he would wait until the thief was caught for his share, while Fouquet said it was the least the Lieutenant could do, and he would have every penny that was due to him. In the end both were persuaded to take the money and having seen it paid to them M. Estoban left.

After he had called at the apothecary's house and was on his way home he wondered if it were the boredom of prison life that turned some men into beasts, while other, simpler folk survived to become less of an animal under the same circumstances.

Both of these men, he reflected sadly, were children of the Revolution, as was the Lieutenant. In their childhood they must have known the overwhelming greed for possessions and money that had swept their parents off their feet and his own family to their deaths, and yet they appeared to have learned no lesson from it.

Not having set foot in France since the emigration that was the immediate forerunner of the Terror, it still did not occur to M. le Comte d'Estoban that he and his friends and the King they had served might also have been equally responsible, with the rabble that they despised and hated, for the Revolution that had taken hold of France.

The apothecary pronounced the wound in Philippe's head

to be a nasty one, advised a compress for the bruises and said that after a few days' rest and careful bathing twice a day he should take no harm. After he had gone the Comte stayed a few minutes by the Lieutenant's bed to tell him about his interview with the Agent and the discharging of his debt to the two prisoners. He ended up by saying:

'Captain Buller has been good enough to grant you a period of leave, and I shall be pleased, Monsieur, if you will consider yourself to be my guest as long as the apothecary thinks fit.'

'I am very much obliged to you, M. le Comte.'

The Comte shrugged. 'You are my countryman.'

After a moment Philippe said, 'You say that you saw Lecointre and Fouquet, Monsieur?'

'I saw them, I spoke to them, and the Agent paid them the money in front of me, and permit me to say that of the two I found your servant Lecointre to be the pleasanter fellow.'

'Gaston is a good man.'

'The man Fouquet is an ungrateful dog, and yet there is something strange about him as well. Captain Buller made them sign a receipt for the money, a wise precaution I have no doubt, but whereas your servant, Lecointre, could only make his mark on the paper, Fouquet signed his name with no trouble at all. One would think he had an education of a sort. Were both men in the army then?'

'No, Monsieur. They were on one of the ships captured by the English at the time when the Emperor had plans for invading England. No doubt you will have heard about it: there were scores of flat-bottomed boats filling every port on the Channel coast, with thousands of men waiting to man them directly the weather permitted. But unfortunately it was not only the weather that did not allow the invasion to take place. The Emperor had not reckoned on the fact that the English held supremacy on the sea, and these English frigates and sloops waited outside our ports like hawks waiting for a mouse to show itself. More than once they had the audacity to raid our shipping on dark nights, sinking them and taking our crews prisoner. It was on one such raid on Boulogne that Lecointre and Fouquet were taken.'

The Comte smiled ironically. 'It is the habit of men like your Emperor, one would think, to underestimate their enemies.'

Philippe Cadot flushed, annoyed by the old man's coldness. 'I would not say that it is a failing peculiar to one man alone, M. le Comte.'

M. Estoban did not stoop to argue with one of Bonaparte's men. He bowed slightly and went to the door. 'My servant will bring you your dinner,' he said. 'We fare better down here than some of the émigrés in London. We do not starve and you will have fresh vegetables with your soup.'

'And did none of the labourers on your estates starve then in the past, you proud old man?' thought Philippe angrily. 'It is convenient to forget such things under your own misfortunes no doubt.' He was glad that he did not see the Comte again for the best part of a week: he felt that if he had to endure much of his conversation he might have committed the unpardonable crime of being impolite to his host.

That evening when Jeanne brought her master's dinner to him in the little dining-room, she found him strangely silent and presently she broke off her chatter to accuse him: 'You are thinking of . . . *that* again, Monsieur! . . . Something has reminded you of it!'

'Yes.' He tried to rouse himself but his smile was sad. 'It was one of those prisoners today – the one who could write his name. He signed it with a flourish, Arblon Fouquet. I was startled to see the name of Arblon, because as you know my daughter-in-law was the daughter of the Marquis d'Arblon. I said, "That is a good name you have there,' and he looked up with such fury and hatred in his face that if the Agent had not been there I think he would have spat at me. "My mother," he said, "was servant to a cursed aristocrat before she married my father, and she gave me their damned name".'

'The animal!' Jeanne was indignant. 'You should have

allowed the man Buller to deal with these beasts, Monsieur. It would have been more dignified.'

'And yet a man may arrive at nothing by clinging to his dignity, ma bonne. The thought came into my mind then, as always at such times, that I might perhaps discover in that uncompromising material, something that might lead me to my grand-son.'

Jeanne put his soup in front of him with a clatter that nearly sent it into his lap. 'Monsieur le Comte,' she said sharply, 'you know how much I love your family. You know that my heart broke as yours did when we heard what had happened. But that little boy is gone, Monsieur. That is a fact that one must accept. It is twenty years now and if he were alive still you must have heard of it from somebody. Nobody would keep you in ignorance. They would have heard and they would have told you.'

'Yes.' The Comte sighed and began his soup. 'As I have said many times before this I have no doubt that you are correct in what you say. You are a good soul, Jeanne.'

But although Jeanne had dismissed the thing with her customary impatience the thought of the prisoner's unusual name stayed with her and gave her a restless night.

Supposing the man's mother should happen to know something of what had happened to the child? It was a chance in a hundred, but it might be there . . .

And then she remembered the stories about poor little Louis XVII and she knew that such chances were very remote indeed. For even if the child had lived to grow up it was more than likely that he would have developed into just such another as this monster Fouquet, with his hand against every man, and if that were so, surely it would be far better if he were never found.

# 7

The story of the attack upon the Lieutenant and the part
played in his recovery by Melissa and young Lady Tamporley
was soon all over the town, and everywhere they went Miss
Cheriton and her niece were surrounded by eager questioners,
while carriages drove out to Tamporley and scented notes
arrived at M. Estoban's little house to enquire after the popular
Lieutenant, until the old émigré remarked drily that he had no
idea that one of Bonaparte's lieutenants could be so popular in
an English town.

The Dowager, remembering the Lieutenant's handsome
face said that she was horrified to think that an Englishman could attack a man like that, but here she was taken to
task by her son.

'For the labouring classes in England today,' he reminded
her, 'food is scarce and dear, and there must be many an
honest fellow who has seen the great loads of meat and flour
and bread going into the Castle for the prisoners there, and
thought of his own family and remembered that he had not
bread to put into the children's mouths . . . No wonder some
of them hate these Frenchmen, making money so easily with
toys that are bought up by the rich, who would do better in
my opinion if they employed more of their own countrymen
in such trades. I cannot help it if I dislike these foreigners,
Mamma. I find it hard even to be pleasant to M. Estoban at
times.'

'Now, Tam, you are not to say one word against the Comte.

He is a sweet old man, and nobody could blame him if he were permanently embittered after the terrible tragedy in his life.'

Her son reminded her in a shout that it all happened a long time ago and it was time they began to forget.

'I daresay it is, dear, but twenty years would never be long enough for me to forget, if you and dear Sarah and all the sweet children had been murdered by those wretches. I can never think of it without shuddering.'

'In the Comte's case I have always thought it to be largely his own fault and the fault of his two sons for rushing off as they did to join Condé's army, leaving their women-folk unprotected. Oh, I know they thought it safe enough and I daresay it would have made no difference in the end, but I would not like to have it on my conscience . . . At that time it would have been much safer for them all to come to Tamporley. You know my father's generosity: old friends as they were, no doubt he would have made over the entire East Wing to them!' And having delivered this opinion in a voice that made his mother's head ring he went off to conclude the purchase of the new chestnut filly with its owner on the other side of Doverton. Her mouth was like silk and her manners were perfect, and after trying her out he thought that even Sarah might be persuaded to ride her without mishap.

For the best part of a week old Jeanne had taken entire charge of the Lieutenant and put off callers by telling them that he was asleep. With great perseverance however Mr. Beaumont succeeded in getting past her one day when the Comte was out in his little chaise, and he climbed the stairs to see the Frenchman for himself, and left shortly afterwards considerably shocked at what he had seen. It was evident that the blow on the head had been more severe than originally thought, and moreover it was obvious that the Lieutenant's bed had not been made for days, and neither had he been washed or shaved. The Frenchman was so glad to see him that it looked as if all visitors had been deliberately excluded from his room, but he spoke in such a weak voice and with such an evident effort that his friend was deeply apprehensive for him.

Happening to meet young Lady Tamporley in the town that morning he told her how concerned he was. 'I am very much afraid that the Lieutenant is not being cared for or nursed as well as he should be,' he said.

'But my housekeeper has sent down beef tea, minced chicken, custards and brandy jellies – all the things that an invalid needs – every day!' protested her gentle little ladyship 'I did not want M. Estoban to be embarrassed by a visitor that I had thrust upon him.'

'I wonder if Cadot has had any of the things your housekeeper sent then, Lady Tamporley?' said Mr. Beaumont.

'But what could have happened to them?' Sarah remembered old Jeanne's hatred for the French heirs to the Revolution. 'She cannot be executing a kind of private vengeance upon poor Mr. Cadot, can she?' she said.

'Perhaps the apothecary was mistaken,' said Mr. Beaumont in a worried tone. 'There may be more serious damage to the head than he thought.'

'I will go and see Mr. Cadot this afternoon,' said Sarah decidedly. 'And if I think it necessary he shall be removed to Tamporley Park.' She drove on while Mr. Beaumont walked on to the library where he was to meet Miss Sophy, and he found that plain young lady waiting for him there and passing the time in conversation with Melissa and one of the young officers of the militia from the Castle.

'I have been telling Miss Forsett that Captain Woodcock and I are old friends,' said Melissa gaily. 'We were childhood sweethearts, were we not, Frank?'

'We were indeed.' But the young man looked a trifle sheepish as he met Mr. Beaumont's smiling eyes, and Melissa, catching a glance that passed between Sophy and the gentlemen, said rather hurriedly that she must fetch the second volume of her book.

'My aunt has been persuaded to read *The Mysteries of Udolpho*,' she explained. 'And we are forgetting our work every night in our breathless interest in the story. We left Valancourt last night tearing himself away from Emily and now we are eagerly awaiting to begin Volume Two.'

She smiled at them and moved away, half-expecting Frank to follow her but he did not. Perhaps he had not noticed the radiance that was on Sophy's face that morning, turning her from a plain young woman into one that was almost handsome. 'Love,' thought Melissa wistfully, 'will do wonderful things for a girl.' She reached up to take the second volume of *Udolpho* from the shelf, but it was too high for her and at the same moment a hand came over her shoulder and a voice said quietly, 'Allow me, Miss Melissa,' and Edward Beaumont put the book into her hand.

'Oh!' She felt herself blushing scarlet in her surprise. 'Thank you . . . ' She glanced at the others but Sophy seemed to be engrossed in something that Captain Woodcock was telling her and Melissa thought that this was an opportunity that she could not miss. She might never have the chance to speak to Edward Beaumont alone again. She said breathlessly, 'Mr. Beaumont, I am glad I have met you again here in Doverton. I have wanted to say how sorry I am for the way I behaved to you last Christmas. I don't know what made me behave as I did, I don't really.'

His smiling eyes met hers with disconcerting unconcern. 'High spirits,' he told her consolingly. 'That was the cause of it, Miss Melissa, and believe me I did not blame you for it in the least. It was entirely my fault: I should have realised that I was a great deal too old to pay serious attentions to a young lady of your age. Please think no more about it. Once I had got over the hurt to my pride, which did not last longer than it took me to remove myself from the district, I never gave the matter a second thought.'

And then young Halstead came in to roar out that he could not keep his cattle waiting a moment more and Edward Beaumont had to give his arm to Sophy and go. Frank accompanied Melissa back to her aunt's house, talking gaily as they went.

'What a charming girl Miss Forsett is!' he said. 'I have met her several times at the Halsteads.'

'She has a charming fortune too,' Melissa could not help remarking sourly. She wished she had felt comforted by Edward Beaumont's assurance that her past unkindness had left no lasting mark on him, but she could not. She could only feel anger and indignation and – yes – grief, that he had contrived to throw off so lightly the enchantment she had cast over him.

'But Miss Sophy and her fortune are both guarded by her fire-eating father and a dragon of an aunt,' said Frank with a wicked little smile. 'Have you not heard about it?'

Melissa said she had, and that as the aunt in question was her cousin's mother-in-law, all her sympathies were with Sophy. 'I daresay though, that not even Mrs. Forsett will object to Mr. Beaumont,' she added.

'Oh, he is the favoured suitor,' agreed Frank, and laughed again, more gaily than before. 'He is invited there at all times and pursued so outrageously that I wonder the poor fellow does not take to his heels and run away!'

Melissa felt her heart sink into her shoes, and she scarcely heard the Captain's next question so that he had to repeat it. 'I asked you if you knew how Lieutenant Cadot is progressing?'

'Why, do you know him?' Melissa was surprised.

'Of course I know him. He is a charming fellow. We play cards together when we are both short of money . . . Philippe is one of my greatest friends.'

A few days ago Melissa might have agreed with Frank that Mr. Cadot was one of the most charming young men she had ever met, but now her thoughts were captured and her heart made heavy by a pair of coldly smiling grey eyes that had told her so plainly that there was no possibility of doubt, that her schoolgirl flirtation of last Christmas meant no more to Edward Beaumont than the breaking of a straw.

\*　　\*　　\*

Sarah drove home by way of Tamporley village, and as she arrived at the Comte's cottage she saw one of the Tamporley footmen arriving with a large covered basket on his arm.

She told the groom to hold the horse while she carried the basket in herself.

'But m'lady, it is heavy,' protested the footman.

'Then you shall carry it for me and we will go into the house together,' said Sarah smiling.

Jeanne, who answered the door to them, told her in a hurry that her master was out.

'So much the better,' said Sarah firmly. 'Because I have come to see M. Cadot and not M. le Comte.'

Jeanne looked flustered and made an unsuccessful attempt to take the basket from the footman. 'It is not seemly, miladi,' she protested.

'Nonsense,' said Sarah, her eyes sparkling. 'I go everywhere in Tamporley and into every house when I am visiting the sick. You will take me upstairs at once to the Lieutenant's room, if you please.'

'Pardon, miladi?' Jeanne pretended not to understand and 'miladi' repeated her request firmly and in excellent French, her gentleness disappearing under a tone of command that the old woman had never heard from her before. 'You will take me upstairs at once,' she said crisply, 'and when you have done that you will heat the soup in this jug and you will bring it upstairs to the Lieutenant with the other things that my housekeeper has sent for him. I will sit with him while he eats them.'

'He will eat nothing, miladi.' But Sarah could see the old woman was frightened in spite of her defiant attitude.

'We will see about that.' Young Lady Tamporley turned to the footman with the basket. 'Go into the kitchen, Albert, and see that my orders are carried out, and directly M. le

6　　　　81

Comte comes in please tell him that I would like to see him immediately.'

This threat had the desired effect. Sullenly Jeanne took her up the stairs and having left her at the Lieutenant's door scuttled down again to the kitchen, where she was followed by the stolid Albert with the basket of food.

Sarah looked with disgust at the unswept room, the unmade bed, and the remains of an untouched meal of dry bread and cold, greasy soup by the bed. She guessed at once that this was Jeanne's doing: no doubt the good old émigré had left the care and the nursing of the injured man to her.

She sat down beside the bed and waited for the Frenchman to awake, and when at last he opened heavy eyes it was to see her there, her face under its rose-coloured bonnet looking like a flower that had somehow strayed into the room by mistake.

'Did you come on a sunbeam?' he asked, attempting to smile at her. 'Angels do not visit rooms like mine . . .'

'Monsieur Cadot!' She spoke gently. 'Has M. Estoban been to see you since you came up to this room?'

'Not after the first day, but that does not matter. The old servant does her best, and when I am fit to crawl from my bed I shall return to the Castle.' He spoke hoarsely and with evident effort.

'They will certainly look after you better there one would think!' She looked around her indignantly. 'It is scandalous that old Jeanne has behaved like this to you.'

'She did her best,' he repeated, but it was obvious when she brought up a tray on which were hot broth, custard and brandy jelly and crisp white bread and butter that she had been doing far from her best. The Lieutenant gazed at the tray as if he could not believe his eyes. 'This is not for me!' he said. 'This has been brought for M. le Comte, Madame. There has been some mistake.'

'There is no mistake,' said Sarah quietly. 'You are to eat it all.' She put the cup of broth into his hands and helped him to take it to his mouth, supporting his hands as she would have done little James's hands had he been ill in bed, and the clasp of her light fingers over his were like the clasp of a saint, lifting his spirit. He felt as if somehow he had strayed into heaven, with an angel waiting on him, and he would have choked down the dry crusts and the cold soup if she had promised to stay.

And she did stay there with him, not speaking much except to persuade him to take another mouthful, and when the food was finished at last she smoothed his pillows and helped him to lie there more comfortably, resting her cool hand on his brow for a moment to see that he was not feverish before she went. The touch of it remained with him so that he slept again almost immediately.

Sarah went downstairs to the old woman in the kitchen. 'When the Lieutenant awakes again,' she said, 'you will take a broom and a duster and clean his room. I would not like M. le Comte to see it as it is, although in its present condition it might explain to him why I am having the Lieutenant removed to Tamporley Park today.'

'Oh, miladi . . . ' Jeanne began to cry into her apron. 'He will send me back to France if you tell him . . . He will be so angry.'

'But I am angry, too,' said Sarah, looking as stern as her sweet face permitted. 'I cannot understand why you have been so cruel, and to one of your own countrymen too.' She paused, and then, as Jeanne went on weeping, relented a little. 'Very well, I will leave M. Cadot here, but I will visit him tomorrow and I shall hope to find him a great deal better than he is today. For shame, Jeanne, to behave like this, not only to that helpless young man upstairs, but to M. le Comte. What will his English friends think of him, when they visit his guest in a dirty room, with food beside him that not even a pig would touch?'

After he had gone Jeanne went quietly upstairs with clean water and sheets for the Lieutenant's bed, and scarcely waited for him to wake before she started to clean the room. As she worked however, she talked to herself, a sorrowful muttering that only half-penetrated the Lieutenant's consciousness.

' "Put him in the unoccupied room," says M'sieu le Comte. But he knows why we have it unoccupied, just in case his grand-son should be found . . . But we shall never find him now. He was lost in The Terror and he will never be found again. M'sieu le Comte thinks so too, that is plain, or else he would never have put one of Bonaparte's men in this room . . . Have I not scoured and scrubbed and kept it ready all these years? And for what? For this young monster? . . . She will tell M'sieu le Comte, will she, this grand English lady? But she does not understand . . . she will never understand because she has not been through the things that I have been through . . . That open boat and the poor old Madame . . . "I am well, Jeanne," she says, shuddering and sick with cold. "Think nothing of me. Look to M'sieu Henri . . . " And when we arrive at last with no money, and have to live in that dreadful little room where we all starve, and M'sieu Henri dies . . . and then Madame dies . . . and M'sieu le Comte comes desperate, half-crazed with grief for his family . . . for his little grand-son . . . "The only one left, Jeanne," he says, "and I cannot find him. If I go to France to look for him there is a price on my head and I shall be arrested the moment I land" . . . All these things have I known, all these things have I endured, my heart breaking for them all . . . for the little boy in France . . . And then they say, "Do this, Jeanne . . . do that, Jeanne . . . " and for what? Tell me that if you please! For an officer of Bonaparte's . . . '

Philippe moved, the bed creaked, and the muttering ceased. The hands that held the scrubbing brush stopped their work, and Jeanne got up on her feet and came to the bed and stared down at him.

'You find yourself better for that good food?' she asked shrilly.

'Thank you, Madame.' He looked up at her with puzzled

eyes. 'Tell me one thing,' he said, 'what makes you so certain that only aristocrats perished in The Terror?'

'And did they not then?'

'Certainly not.' He frowned, trying to put his thoughts in order but his head seemed to be full of clouds, on which a face with golden hair and a pink velvet bonnet rested with angelic sweetness. 'My parents were not aristocrats,' he said. 'They were bourgeois and good republicans, and yet they perished in the same way.'

'By . . . the guillotine, parbleu?' Jeanne drew closer, the enmity in her black eyes lessening a little.

'Of course. My uncle was nearly caught himself when he went back to Paris to fetch me and take me to my aunt in the country.'

'Do you remember it then?' Jeanne poured some of the water into the basin on the table and began to wash his face gently. 'I will have the barber to shave you tomorrow when he has finished with M'sieu le Comte . . . How old were you at the time?'

'Four or five perhaps . . . which is why I remember very little of it all. I seem to recollect roads full of people, all moving in one direction . . . and carriages . . . and once a diligence, with everybody talking and nobody listening, and that feeling of fear . . . That I *do* remember! . . . The feeling of fear. Everybody was frightened, Madame, everybody . . . '

Jeanne understood very well. In her turn she told him about the Comte d'Estoban, the last of his family, and how he had joined Condé's army. 'It was an army intended to liberate the King,' she went on sorrowfully, 'but nothing came of it, I don't know why. Some said it was because it was a gentleman's army, composed of gentlemen who had no idea of fighting and no notion how to plan a campaign. Who can say? In the event M'sieu le Comte's elder son, M'sieu Adolphe, died of fever, and his brother M'sieu Auguste, who was only sixteen, was killed in a duel, and only M. le Comte was left to follow the prince until the so-called army was disbanded

85

and M'sieu fled to England . . . He had left Madame la Comtesse and his daughter, Mademoiselle Thérèse, who was seventeen, and Madame Adolphe and her little boy of four years old in the château, thinking they would be safe there. The estate was a large one and there were many servants, all devoted to the family, because M'sieu le Comte was a good man, you understand. He was good to his servants, and to the villagers on his estate, not like some of these . . . the Marquis d'Arblon, for example. There was one who was hated and with reason . . . It was said that if there was a pretty young woman in one of his villages and he happened to want her, he would see to it that the men in her family were taken up for not paying their taxes, and sent away to make the roads on the other side of the country, so that there was none left in the village to save her from him. But marquis as he was, M'sieu le Comte took precedent over him because he had the right to ride in the King's carriage . . . For generations the Estobans had this right, you understand. And with reason, because they were all men who could be trusted and loved.'

She paused, using a clean towel to wipe his face gently, her thoughts far away.

'What happened then?' he asked at last. 'To the ladies . . . '

'One day that summer we heard that a rabble several thousand strong were marching on the château, intent on burning it to the ground . . . Well, you may argue with a score perhaps, and tell them that they are mistaken, but you cannot argue with a thousand, M'sieu! Madame la Comtesse ordered carriages to be got ready and she and the family left the Hôtel d'Estoban in Paris. There were three carriages, and we all got separated because the roads were thronged with refugees. You can have no real idea what it was like, because as you say, you were too young to remember, but it was as you said, everybody flying in one direction, towards Paris, carriages, farm carts, fine ladies on foot, their beautiful slippers cut to ribbons, men and women carrying bundles of clothes and food, with small children hanging on to their skirts, and over them all that feeling of fear. Madame la Comtesse and Madame Adolphe and Mademoiselle Thérèse were in the first carriage, with Mademoiselle's *gouvernante*, and in the second carriage there was the little boy and his nurse and such clothing and food that they would need for the night, and the ladies' maids with the cases of jewellery. The little boy had been ill and it was thought there would be more room for him to sleep on the journey. The last carriage held a few of us servants and what clothing and valuables we had managed to save. But when we arrived at nightfall on the second day at a village where we felt it would be safe to rest, the middle carriage had disappeared. We had been going through wooded country, with many hills, and somehow it had got separated from the others. Nobody had seen it go, nobody knew what had become of it. But it was thought that in the dusk the coachman had taken a wrong turning, mistaking another carriage for ours, and had followed it for a way until he discovered his mistake. Madame Adolphe was for turning back, but, mon dieu, how could one turn back on those crowded roads? Madame la Comtesse promised her that we should find the second carriage waiting for us in Paris, or that they would not be far behind. She was quite sure, as we all were, that the coachman would find his way there with the rest. But when we all arrived at the Hôtel d'Estoban in the Faubourg St. Germain the child and his nurse had not arrived, and neither did they arrive later. From that day, in fact, M'sieu, nothing has been heard of them or the ladies' maids and the jewellery.'

'But was the carriage not found? That is a large thing to vanish surely?'

'And who was there to go looking for it at that time? The few servants who had remained to defend the château were killed, the rest had fled, Madame la Comtesse, her daughter, Mademoiselle Thérèse, and Madame Adolphe, no sooner arrived in Paris when they were told that they must not leave the house. It was known by then that M. le Comte and his two sons had joined the Prince Condé's army you see, and the ladies were held under the pretext that they were spies.'

'But that was absurd.'

'Naturally. But after they had been confined to their Hôtel for six months or more they were taken off to prison one morning, and soon afterwards all were executed on the guillotine, even little Mademoiselle Thérèse and her *gouvernante*.'

'Those were terrible days, Madame.'

'Terrible indeed, M'sieu. I used to think I was being followed whenever I stepped outside the door . . . I waited for a hand on my shoulder and a voice accusing me of being "One of those from the Hôtel d'Estoban . . . " And then old M'sieu Henri d'Estoban and his wife sent for me and I came with them to England . . . ' She paused. By this time she had remade his bed and clothed him in a clean nightshirt, and had beaten up his pillows so that he could lean back on them in comfort, and when this was done she said, changing the subject rather abruptly: 'This man Fouquet at the Castle here, M'sieu, the one who made the little ship, what is he? . . . For example, what is his father?'

'I think Gaston told me that he was a dealer in secondhand furniture and clothes, Madame.'

'Ah!' She nodded significantly. 'That does not surprise me. No doubt he did a brisk trade at one time, then, and no doubt there were silk dresses and velvet coats going in his shop for a few sous, and brocaded furniture and gentlemen's swords, to be sold to the metal-dealers . . . I understand very well what Fouquet's father was . . . No wonder he could afford to have his son taught to write!'

And then, having finished with his room and himself, she went away downstairs and left him to continue his sleep, but both of them were aware of a new sympathy and a bond between them, because at much the same time they and their families must have been travelling the same, congested, terror-stricken roads to Paris, some to find a fleeting success there, others to find imprisonment, and most of them in the end to tread the same path to the guillotine and death.

That evening she told the Comte: 'That young man of ours upstairs has more understanding than one would think . . . He tells me that his parents also died during The Terror. No doubt they deserved their fate, but I daresay there were some good ones among the so-called republicans after all.'

'As there were bad among us,' said the Comte smiling. 'Has he planted this poison in your mind too, ma bonne?'

'Indeed he did not,' she said tossing her head indignantly. 'He had better try!'

The Comte said no more, but after she had left him he thought of the young man upstairs and felt a fleeting compassion for his parents . . . No doubt it was only justice that had sent them to the guillotine, but he was sorry that they had not lived to see their son grow up. Nobody could deny that he was a handsome young man.

Then, as the shadows crept into the salon his thoughts suddenly went back to a summer's day when he had been the age that Philippe Cadot was now. He had been down in the country hunting with some young friends, and as they came home they rode their horses, laughing, through a field of standing corn, while the man who had planted and tended it, and looked to it to feed his family and provide the tithe that was due, stood leaning on his hoe watching them and saying nothing, but with the tears streaming down his face.

The March evening was chilly and M. le Comte d'Estoban drew closer to his fire, holding out his delicate hands to the warmth as if he were suddenly cold.

# 8

Jeanne's changed attitude towards the Lieutenant had such
an excellent effect on his health and his spirits that by the
end of another four days he was able to come downstairs,
and was invited – nay commanded – to play chess with M.
Estoban in the sanctity of the salon.

Mindful of the honour that was being shown to him Philippe
was careful to allow the old gentleman to defeat him, but as
adversaries over the chessboard they began to find an apprecia-
tion of each other that constantly surprised them.

To Philippe, brought up to hold the old régime in con-
tempt, and taught from his childhood that these people had
regarded the men and women on their estates as so much
livestock, there came small moments of astonishment to hear
the old man declaim, 'As I used to say to my farmers sometimes . . . ' as if he had been accustomed to discussing affairs
with them on terms of equality on the rare occasions when
he had been able to escape from The Court at Versailles. And
to the Comte, who had all his life dismissed republicans as
fools or knaves, there came moments when admiration forced
itself upon him for his young guest's sincerity and honesty,
even if there were subjects on which they would always be
poles apart.

'Am I to understand then, Monsieur,' he asked him one
day, 'that you studied at one of the lycées in Paris before you
were called into the army?'

'But yes, M. le Comte.'

'And what did you study there, for example?'

'Literature, ancient and modern, the mathematical and physical sciences, as they apply to general life and to the professions, and of course modern languages.'

'And how long did it take you to acquire such knowledge and in so many branches?' If the Comte's voice held irony the Lieutenant did not notice it.

'Six years was the time fixed for it, M. le Comte, but I did not complete the course because I was called into the army before I finished. It was not thought that my profession was important enough to allow me to complete my studies.'

'And what was that profession then?'

'The same as my father, Monsieur – that of the law.'

'Ah yes, of course. You told me.' The Comte thought it a pity that so bourgeois a profession had been selected, but then all professions were bourgeois, when one came to think about it. He sighed and reminded Phillipe that he was waiting for him to play.

\*　　\*　　\*

The children at Tamporley in the meantime were eager to meet Miss Cheriton's Romantic Frenchman and to hear from his own lips the full story of his adventure on the Heath, and when Sarah was assured that he was strong enough to stand such an invasion, she asked Miss Pope's permission to take them down to visit the Comte and his invalid. Miss Pope was always happy for the children to visit the old émigré: she declared that his French was so good for their pronunciation, but Sarah had a shrewd suspicion that the old gentleman's compliments won the governess's heart.

It was of course unthinkable that Sarah should visit the Frenchman with her children without her partner in the adventure being present, and once again a carriage and a note were despatched to Miss Cheriton's little house, and this time Miss

Cheriton took the opportunity of accompanying her niece, to see for herself how her favourite was progressing.

Sarah and the governess and the children were to walk down through the park, but as Miss Cheriton and her niece arrived in the carriage they found that Mr. Beaumont had been sitting with Philippe upstairs while the barber shaved him, and while Sophy Forsett had her weekly French lesson with the Comte.

There was in fact no need at all for Miss Sophy to learn French from the Comte: she spoke it excellently already. But it gave her the opportunity to visit Jeanne in the kitchen on her way out, knowing that M. Estoban was far too proud to charge for his services, and to slip some money under a vase that stood on the kitchen chimney piece. Nobody mentioned this small transaction, least of all Miss Sophy herself: she was a kindly, tender-hearted girl, and she felt it was all she could do towards the comfort of the old émigré.

Philippe was handsomer than ever as he followed Mr. Beaumont downstairs and bowed over Melissa's hand and her aunt's, complimenting them in his usual flowery way on their looks and their dresses. He had an interesting pallor in his face, and the bandage that still ornamented his cropped, curly head gave him an even more romantic look. And when Sophy came out of the little salon with her lesson completed and the Comte took up the compliments where Philippe had left off, Melissa thought sourly that the younger Frenchman's greeting to Miss Sophy was as exaggerated as if she had been the prettiest girl in the district. She remembered Tam's remarks about the French officers in Doverton, and that they would be serious over no English girl unless she had money, and she glanced at Mr. Beaumont to see how he was taking this meeting between his new friend and the girl who was the object of his visit to Dove Tye. But he was gravely smiling as he listened to Philippe's nonsense, and when Jeanne came to tell them her ladyship and the children were approaching across the rustic bridge, everyone had to go out to welcome them, so that for a moment Mr. Beaumont was alone with Melissa. He could not help remarking with a whimsical little smile that Philippe Cadot was a sad fellow for the ladies. Melissa agreed with him.

'He pays them all such elaborate compliments,' she added. 'Even the plain ones . . .'

He studied her thoughtfully, and he did not pretend not to understand her meaning. 'But then none of Miss Sophy's friends could think her plain,' he remarked. 'Her face reflects her nature, which is one of the most charming I have ever encountered in a young woman of her age.'

'Oh dear!' thought Melissa. 'The wind *does* sit in that quarter indeed!' Aloud she had to agree once more while inwardly she could have wept.

Philippe Cadot, standing with the Comte and Miss Cheriton and Sophy in Jeanne's little garden, watched the Tamporley group approaching. Naturally when they reached the bridge the children had to look for the fish that could be seen there sometimes, darting from stone to stone in the clear water, and the three-year-old James stooped to pick some celandines that were out under the golden tresses of a weeping willow, crooning to himself as he did so, while his mother watched him tenderly.

Philippe thought how charming the little group was, with the gentle little mother and the five children: even the thin, black-clad governess added something to it by contrast. But his eyes were inescapably drawn to Sarah and rested on her face, and no empty compliments came to his mind at that moment. He simply thought with bitter envy of her husband, that large, loud-voiced, unappreciative Englishman, and he wondered how any man in his senses could accept Sarah as his wife and not thank God for her every hour of his day.

And then she was there in the garden, with her hand held out to him, smiling up at him as he took it to his lips, asking how he did in the meantime and saying how pleased she was to see him so much better, and all in her breathless, soft little voice, while the older children were made by their governess to greet the Comte in a civilised fashion, instead of dancing round him like savages.

At first when they were introduced to the Lieutenant they were dumb with shyness, but once their tongues were loosened by his friendliness they all began talking at once. What was the robber like, they wanted to know? Was he big and black-haired and rough, like a gipsy? Did the wound hurt? Did it bleed a great deal? How much blood was there did he think? And was he very frightened? For a time it was impossible for their mother, their governess or Melissa to guide the conversation into less gory channels, and Sophy said that she would go before the details of M. Cadot's attack made her feel sick. She could not even look at the picture of a battle, she added, without feeling faint.

'Then, Mademoiselle Sophy,' said Philippe gravely, 'it is quite plain that you should never marry a soldier.'

Sophy laughed, with a joyous lilt in her laughter, and Melissa thought unhappily that this plain duckling had indeed learned to spread her wings. She caught a glance that passed between Sophy and the Lieutenant and Mr. Beaumont and was reminded of a similar moment in the library when Frank Woodcock had been there and did not know what to make of it at all. 'Now what makes you think, M. Cadot,' said Sophy, 'that I would ever do a thing like that?'

'Everything is possible, Mademoiselle,' said Philippe, gallantly, 'where a lady like yourself is concerned.'

'I will leave you to the children,' she said laughing. 'It is only what you deserve!' And then Edward Beaumont swept her off to his chaise and drove her home to Dove Tye while the Lieutenant submitted himself to the children's questions.

'But certainly the robber was big and as strong as a lion,' he told them. 'Although I did not see him because, voyez, he attacked me from the rear. But certainly the wound hurt. Mon dieu, your Mamma will tell you that when she and Miss Melissa came upon me in your Papa's park I was screaming in agony . . . Did I not scream, Mademoiselle Melissa? Tell them then.'

'Oh yes, no doubt he screamed.' Melissa joined in the game

although she found that she did not like the Lieutenant as much as before. 'Of course we did not hear him, because he had stopped before we arrived.'

'And had I not bled copiously? Were there not pools of blood around me, enough to fill Jeanne's wash-tub?'

'But of course, Monsieur . . . ' And then M. Estoban remarked that he did not wish his visitor to be fatigued with too much conversation and ordered Philippe to rest himself on the chaise-longue in the salon while he called Jeanne to fetch eau sucré for the children and chocolate for the ladies.

Melissa accompanied her aunt in to the Comte's little dining-parlour where he exhibited once more his musical box, a joy that never failed to enchant the Tamporley children, and he courteously invited Miss Pope to go with them, so that they might conduct a French lesson together, and thus feel that the morning had not been wasted. Sarah found herself alone with the Lieutenant, and had the odd feeling that she had known him all her life.

'Is not M. Estoban charming?' she asked.

'He is a good old man,' he replied. 'A gentle old man, although at first his exquisite politeness made me feel an unmannerly boor. But he has forgiven me now for being one of the Emperor's soldiers and he treats me like an honoured guest.'

'And Jeanne? I hope she is behaving better than she did?'

'Oh yes. Madame and I are the best of friends.'

'And she is no longer throwing away the food that is sent for you?'

'On the contrary, she is stuffing me with it as if I were a prize pig ready for next week's market!' He smiled into her eyes. 'I have not thanked you enough for all you have done for me, Lady Tamporley, but the thanks are here . . . in my heart.'

Her eyes met his shiningly. 'But if it were my little James grown up, I would like to feel that somebody were caring for him in a foreign land.'

'But I am not James,' he said gently. 'I am your age . . . I should not say that you are much more than twenty-five.'

'I am twenty-six, Monsieur.'

'So young? . . . You must have married at an early age?'

'At seventeen.'

'And no doubt you were very much in love with your fine husband . . . I do not think marriages are arranged so much over here as they are at home in France?'

'In a way they are not . . . And yet in a way too they *are* arranged. I had always been ruled in everything by my mother, and when she suggested that I should marry Tam I thought it would be wonderful to be Lady Tamporley of Tamporley Park . . . I was easily persuaded that I could be in love with a man, as well as with his title and his estates . . . '

Why was she saying this to a stranger? she wondered. These were the secret things that she had scarcely dared to tell herself over the years. And yet he was not a stranger to her, this young Frenchman. She felt that she had been waiting for him to arrive, so that she could tell him her inmost thoughts and know that he would understand. She said questioningly, 'In France I expect they arrange things better?'

'But in France young girls are even more strictly kept than they are over here. They are never permitted to be alone with a young man, even if they are affianced . . . ' He studied her serious face with equal gravity. 'But that is not to say that love is not permitted, before and after marriage.'

'After marriage,' she repeated, her soft lips unsmiling. 'But then it is too late . . . '

'No, Madame, you are wrong . . . it is never too late.' His face was as serious as her own, his eyes so dark under their thick lashes that she felt they held only one message for her, and one that she dare not read. She said with a little gasp of relief, 'The music has ceased. Let us go and see what other treasures M. Estoban has found to show the children.'

She hurried out of the room and he got up and followed her more leisurely. The Comte had brought out a toy to amuse his young guests: a small round platform, on which were mounted three little drummers in a uniform of many years ago, and there was a handle in the side of the platform, which, when it was turned, animated the drummers into beating a tattoo on their drums. The children were in ecstasies over it, and had to demonstrate the drummers' performance to each other and to their mother and the Lieutenant, and it was with the greatest reluctance that they consented to be parted from the toy at last, and finished the eau sucré and said goodbye to the Comte.

'You shall come and see it again, my dears,' he told them before they left. 'You know that I would give it to you, but it belonged to a little boy who was very dear to me once. It was the only thing of his that Jeanne saved from my Paris house. And I do not know of any shop in Doverton where your Mamma could buy you one like it. Such toys were all made in France.'

'But I have seen one like it.' Philippe examined the boy drummers with interest, but looking slightly puzzled too. 'I cannot tell you where I saw it, but it was when I was a child . . . In all probability I had one like it at one time. But our prisoners up at the Castle are very clever at making such things.' He turned to Sarah smilingly, the gravity of a few minutes ago gone. 'You should take the children to the prison market one day, Lady Tamporley. Not only are there toys such as this for sale, but we have clowns and tumblers and jugglers there for them to watch – all very amusing.'

'I know. I have heard about it from others.' Sarah's eyes did not meet his. 'But I am afraid my husband would not allow me to take the children there. He says the things the prisoners make are too expensive.'

'But Aunt Charity and I intend to go there one day soon,' said Melissa hastily, seeing the words, "And Papa hates Frenchmen" trembling on the eldest child's lips. 'We saw a beautiful work-box the other day, that one of Aunt Charity's friends bought at your market. Didn't we, Aunt Charity?'

'Why yes.' Miss Cheriton, who had been talking to Jeanne in the kitchen, told her favourite about it. 'It was made of straw-work, Mr. Cadot, and lined with grey silk. I would dearly like to find one like it.'

'So when Aunt Charity goes to the market to look for her work-box,' said Melissa gaily, 'I will look for the children's drummers!'

They say goodbye and left, the children with their governess returning home through the park, and Sarah accompanying her aunt and Melissa in the carriage to the Dower House, where they were to spend the rest of the day.

'Do you know what Jeanne told me, my dears, while I was giving her my recipe for medlar preserve?' said Miss Cheriton round-eyed. 'She told me that one of those men at the prison had the name of Arblong, which is the same as the Comte's daughter-in-law, and that it was because the prisoner's mother had been a servant of the family. I *think* it was Arblong, but I'm not quite sure. I can never remember French names as easily as English ones. They're so foreign, aren't they?'

Melissa asked what man she was talking about.

'Why, the man that made the little ship that the poor Lieutenant was nearly killed for, you know. Fouquet, Jeanne said . . . yes, that was it. Fouquet. I can remember *that* quite easily because it sounds so Chinese, like Tokay, you know. Well, Jeanne says she thinks that perhaps the man might know something about the Comte's family, and what happened to his grand-son in particular, and she was saying that she wished she could approach the man herself.'

'Surely the Comte would not like that?' said Melissa. Sarah said nothing at all: she was staring out of the window at the swinging hazel catkins and the blackthorn that was white beneath them and the bright green of the hawthorn, as if she had never seen them before.

'I told Jeanne not to say a word to him,' said Miss Cheriton nodding her head and smiling mysteriously. 'I had already made up my mind that I would see what I could do.'

'You? But my dearest Aunt, what can you do?'

'When we go to the Castle market I shall see if I can find

this Chinese man,' said her aunt. 'No, I mean the Frenchman with the Chinese name . . . and I will ask him if he knows what happened to the poor little boy.'

'Do you think that would be wise?' Melissa glanced at her cousin's wife for assistance but Sarah was lost in the beauty of the blackthorn, and indeed it was as white as a bridal wreath. 'I'm afraid I have not quite such a high opinion of some of these Frenchmen as I had.'

'Now, Mel, I don't see why you should say that. You have only met our nice Mr. Cadot.'

'And I have more than a notion that your nice Mr. Cadot is pursuing a certain young lady with money.'

'You mean Sophy?' Miss Cheriton was shocked. 'Oh no, dear, it is plain to anyone that Mr. Beaumont is the one that Sophy intends to have, and I hope something will come of it too. I like what I have seen of the gentleman immensely and I am sure that Sophy will make him an excellent wife. I did not think she was looking nearly so plain this morning, did you, Sarah?'

But she had to ask the question three times before young Lady Tamporley heard her and then she apologised, saying that her thoughts had been far away.

'Sophy is in love,' she told her aunt smiling. 'That is why she is looking much prettier than she did.'

Melissa said she was afraid she was, and then she added in a voice that sounded strained in her own ears: 'But is Mr. Beaumont in love with Sophy?'

'Mr. Beaumont is the kind of man who does not reveal his feelings,' said her aunt cheerfully. 'But I am quite sure he would not pay these marked attentions to a girl unless he were in earnest.'

And Melissa, remembering sadly the events of last Christmas, did not reply.

Sarah left them at the Dower House and went on in the carriage to the park. As she got out of the carriage she saw the children following their governess into the house, James, his legs being shorter than the others', trailing behind wearily, the celandines still clutched in his hand.

When he saw her however he forgot his tiredness and ran to her, and she picked him up and hugged him.

'The celandines,' she said as she put him down. He showed them to her anxiously. 'I picked them for you, Mamma, and they're all dead.'

'But they'll revive in water,' she consoled him. 'I love celandines, James.'

'Better than daffodils and violets?' he asked.

Only for a moment she hesitated, then, 'Much better, my love,' she said softly. She took the drooping flowers from him and kissed his hot, grubby little hand before she let him go, and he looked up into her face wonderingly.

'You must love me very much,' he said. 'Because you called me your love.'

'And so you are,' she said. She caught him close again and bent her face to his curly hair to hide the sudden tears in her eyes. 'It is never too late for love,' Philippe Cadot had said. But there were all kinds of love . . . And if you were too late for one kind there were others . . . like James, for instance. Little, dear James . . .

# 9

The prison market was held in the wide road that divided the two stockades within the Castle, twice a week. On Tuesdays and Fridays the stalls that lined the stockades were given over to the inmates who were allowed to exhibit their wares from nine o'clock until two.

On the other days of the week the same stalls were occupied by the produce of small farmers and the tradesmen in the town, selling foodstuffs and needles and thread and pots and pans to the prisoners, and poor quality leather for their shoes. At all times the centre of the road between the North and South Gates was occupied by acrobats, tumblers and jugglers among the prisoners, collecting a few pence by entertaining the farmers' families, and the public who came to buy.

Miss Cheriton wrote to Captain Woodcock to ask him to be so kind as to provide her and her niece with an escort for the following Friday, and when they arrived at the gates that morning they were met by the gallant Captain himself and a young Ensign with a stammer, and were joined before they entered the gates by Mr. Beaumont and Miss Sophy, who always enjoyed a visit to the prison market and had promised her companion a sight of it too.

Unfortunately neither Captain Woodcock nor his young Ensign were able to speak any French, and as Sophy's command of the language was infinitely better than her own, Melissa left her to ask the whereabouts of the stall that held the work-boxes. She stopped beside the first stall inside the

101

gates and asked a man who had list slippers for sale, and was told at once that the work-boxes were beyond the booth that had the performing puppets. 'Punch's Opera it is called,' he said. 'There is a man turning somersaults in front of it, Mademoiselle, and the name on the stall is Cateau. It is written on a card in front of the boxes.'

Sophy thanked him and the party moved on, but it was a fine morning and the market was crowded and somehow Miss Cheriton found herself leading the party with the stammering young Ensign, while Sophy and Captain Woodcock were separated from them in the throng, and his scarlet coat and her smart London bonnet were soon lost among country bonnets and beaver hats and good country broad-cloth.

Melissa found herself alone with Edward Beaumont and as the silence between them became embarrassing, told him hurriedly that she was looking for a toy for the Tamporley children.

'My French is not so good as Sophy's,' she added, 'but as she seems to have been parted from us for the moment I think I had better ask for myself.' They stopped at a stall that had a display of cribbage boards carved in bone, and in her halting French she asked the man there if he knew if there were any mechanical toys for sale.

'Not today, I think, Mademoiselle.' He shook his head. 'The best are made by Arblon Fouquet and I do not think he is here this morning. He is an idle fellow, that one.'

'Arblon Fouquet?' She was startled.

'You know him then?' He smiled with a touch of pride. 'But everyone knows Fouquet! Every man who has something to sell is given a permit to attend this market, otherwise nobody is allowed to be here, and I have not seen him today. I do not think he has made any of these moving toys lately. He has been busy with a ship.'

'So I understand. Lieutenant Cadot sold it for him.'

'Ah! The Lieutenant who was injured by a miscreant. We have all heard of that. How does it go with him, Mademoiselle?'

'He is a great deal better, thank you.'

'C'est bien. He is a good young man, that Lieutenant.'

She turned to relate the conversation to her companion and found that he had understood most of what had been said. 'It is odd how that fellow Fouquet follows us,' he remarked with a wry little smile. 'The Comte could not bear him, so I understand, and Philippe Cadot does not like him either. He says he is a selfish, merciless animal, with his hand against everyone. But I told him that such men are not peculiar to France. There are many like him in every country in the world, thinking only of their own good.'

'Revolutionaries,' said Melissa with a shiver.

'That . . . and worse.'

'Then perhaps it is as well that Fouquet is not here today.' She told him about her aunt's plan for assisting the Comte in his search for his grand-son, and she was glad to see that Edward Beaumont was as much against it as she was.

'Quite apart from the fact that M. Estoban is too proud a man to welcome any outside interference in his private affairs,' he said frowning, 'it would not be wise to put such ideas into the head of a man like this Fouquet. If he should escape at any time he might visit the old man and obtain money from him by saying that he knew where his grand-son was.'

It was unfortunate that at this moment the seller of the cribbage boards recognised Fouquet and cried out to them, that there, coming towards them, was the man they were looking for and before they could prevent him or say that they had changed their minds, he called out to a tall Frenchman in a yellow prison uniform that was a great deal too small for his long limbs, and explained to him in a dialect that Melissa found it hard to follow that she was looking for mechanical toys.

'Mechanical toys? But of course I make them.' Fouquet stopped and started at Melissa so insolently that Mr. Beaumont clenched his fist slowly. 'Perhaps the young lady would like to see my model of the guillotine, with the knife that falls and the heads that fall too into the basket?'

Melissa drew herself up and spoke crisply in his own tongue. 'Although such a toy might make a French child laugh, Monsieur, it would scarcely amuse English children or their relations.'

He looked startled and somewhat taken aback to discover that she had understood his impudence and stood silent and sullen in front of her.

'Can you never learn to hold your tongue, imbecile?' growled the man with the cribbage boards. 'Though if you wish to lose the chance of a sale, who am I to care? It is your concern, parbleu!'

'Miss Melissa,' said Edward Beaumont, 'I don't think it is worth while troubling yourself any further with this man. He has obviously nothing for sale, and if he speaks to you like that again I shall report him to Captain Buller.' He guessed rightly that Fouquet understood English if he did not speak it, and he saw him cringe.

'I beg your pardon, M'sieu,' he said in broken English. 'I not understand what was want . . . I make mistake.'

'You did make a mistake,' said Mr. Beaumont. 'Take care that you do not make another.'

'But no, M'sieu . . . if M'sieu and Mademoiselle come wiz me, my toys over by Sout' Gate.'

'Very well.' The man set off at speed and after a quick glance about him Edward Beaumont prepared to follow him. 'You had better take my arm,' he told Melissa, 'or we shall get parted from each other in this crush.'

'But Sophy . . . ' she began, and saw him smile.

'Miss Sophy is watching the jugglers with Captain Woodcock to see that she comes to no harm,' he said. 'And your aunt has arrived at the stall with the work-boxes. I can see even from this distance that she is hopelessly lost in admiration and cannot make up her mind which one she will have. With any luck we shall have finished our business with Fouquet before she has selected her work-box and the jugglers complete their turn.'

Melissa saw her aunt hovering between boxes covered with straw marquetry, in rolled paper work, and in fine designs like Tunbridge ware. There were linings of grey silk, and of rose colour and of white, and while she hovered and exclaimed and sighed over them the young Ensign stood by her in an attitude of polite but bored attention.

Melissa hesitated no longer. She took Edward Beaumont's arm and they hurried after the long legs of Arblon Fouquet and were soon at his stall. His name was on the front of it on a card that partly hid the model of the guillotine, and he put it aside so that he could demonstrate the gruesome little toy to them, grimly amused to see her shiver and the man beside her frown his displeasure.

'It is well made, Monsieur, but as I said, too horrible for English children.' Melissa's eyes regarded him thoughtfully: he was indeed a Satanic looking creature.

'If Mademoiselle could tell me the sort of thing for which she is searching?' he said with more politeness and schooling his patois to her French.

She described the drummers on their platform and the handle that turned to make them beat their drums, and she saw his eyes light up and he nodded.

'It would be easy to make, that,' he said. 'Were they English drummers, then, Mademoiselle?'

'No, they were French, and dressed in a uniform that you might not recognise because the toy was made about twenty years ago or more.'

'Twenty years ago? Diable, Mademoiselle, I was only five years old at that time. I would not remember such a uniform.'

'No, of course not.' Hastily she examined some of the toys. 'These performing bears are finely made, Monsieur. How much are they? . . . And these poodles . . . '

He told her the price and she was hesitating between the poodles and the bears when Sophy's voice exclaimed beside them, 'So that is where you have got to! . . . You are buying toys . . . And are they not beautifully made? Mr. Beaumont, we have been watching the jugglers. I never visit the Castle market without watching the jugglers. They are so clever, balancing jugs of water and even chairs on their heads . . . ' She broke off. 'And here is Miss Cheriton with her work-box, so we are all together again!'

'I will take the poodles,' said Melissa quickly.

'Very good, Mademoiselle. I will find a box to put them in.'

'Do not trouble. I will take them as they are.' She took her purse from the pocket of her dress and found the money for the toy, but quick as she was, she was not quite quick enough.

'Mel!' cried Miss Cheriton, catching her arm. 'Do you see the man's name on this stall, dear?'

'Yes . . . What a pretty work-box, Aunt Charity! I thought you would choose a straw-work one: they are more unusual. And that rose silk lining is much prettier than the grey . . . '

'Never mind about my work-box, dear. I must ask this man if he knows anything about the Comte's grandson. It is a Heaven-sent opportunity.'

'Aunt Charity, pray don't do anything of the sort.' Melissa lowered her voice. 'I have been talking to Mr. Beaumont about it and he thinks it might be dangerous to take such a man into your confidence.'

'Mr. Beaumont knows nothing about it, Mel. He is quite a stranger to the district.'

'But some of these prisoners hate the French émigrés, and if this man Fouquet should ever come across the poor old Comte he might attack him.' Melissa said the first thing that came into her head and was immediately abused for it.

'I never heard such nonsense in my life. He is one of the ordinary prisoners – from the ranks, dear – and none of these men in yellow uniforms are ever let outside the Castle walls. I know what I am talking about: the regulations are very strict.'

'I daresay they are, but supposing he escaped . . . '

'It is not at all likely, dear! No, Mel, in fairness to the dear Comte I must speak to him. I daresay he will understand English. Some of them do, and he looks an intelligent fellow.'

106

Sophy had momentarily drawn Edward Beaumont's attention to some musical boxes on the next stall and Miss Cheriton appealed to the Captain and his friend. 'Have either of you gentlemen any objection if I put some questions to this prisoner?'

'Of course not, Miss Cheriton.' But Captain Woodcock was not really listening, being also attracted to the musical boxes, and the Ensign was gazing at Melissa, and wondering why she was looking so distressed.

Miss Cheriton approached Fouquet and spoke loudly and clearly as her sister the Dowager did when speaking to foreigners. 'Monsieur Fouquet,' she said, 'no doubt you recall the Comte d'Estoban, who visited you the other day?'

He frowned swiftly. 'Pardon, Madame?' he said disappointingly.

Miss Cheriton repeated her question, speaking more slowly still and this time she saw his lips go down in a sardonic grin.

'A Comte?' he repeated. 'Diable, what should I do wiz zis Comte then? Madame mistake me for aristo, yes?'

Melissa flushed indignantly and was about to implore her aunt once more to come away, when Miss Cheriton stopped her. She saw no insolence in the man: he was, she thought, just amusingly foreign. She went on chattily:

'No doubt you did not think he was a Comte, but he is one of your émigrés, and he was very interested in your name Arblong, because that was the name of his daughter-in-law, poor creature.' She broke off because Melissa, suddenly frightened at the dangerous look of understanding in the man's face, had pulled her sleeve. 'What is it, Mel? I wish you would not interrupt me, dear. I have not finished what I was going to say and you will put it out of my mind.'

Melissa thought it would be an excellent thing if she did but Fouquet had returned to his stall and was arranging a fresh lot of toys in front of the guillotine.

'Bien, Madame, he said evenly, placing toys in which when

handles were turned fiddlers played, and bears danced, and monkeys chased each other's tails, and balls were balanced on the noses of tiny jugglers just as the jugglers did in the yard behind them. 'I sink I remember zis émigré. 'E 'as zis powder in ze 'air and 'e wear zis coat wiz zese vork' buttons of steel...'

'Worked steel buttons. Yes, that is the old gentleman. I knew you would remember him!' Miss Cheriton was delighted. 'The poor old Comte, we are all so sorry for him, and we would like to help him if he could. He lost his two sons with the Prince of Condé's army, you see, and his wife and his daughter and his daughter-in-law the one who was an Arblong, Monsieur, all perished in The Terror.'

'Zat was ver' sad, Madame.' But his smile deepened, and almost absent-mindedly he turned the handle of the little model of the guillotine and behind the performing poodles and the jugglers and the fiddlers and the monkeys the knife crashed down and a tiny head tumbled into the basket. Melissa averted her eyes and waited helplessly for her aunt to continue, and Miss Cheriton, now in full spate, could not have been stayed at that moment by the arrival of the Comte himself. 'It occurred to me in my anxiety to help our dear old friend,' she told him, 'that perhaps you might assist us too.'

'But Madame, 'ow can you zink I would not 'elp an émigré?' The note of sarcasm in his voice was lost upon her and she hurried on:

'The next time you write a letter home, Monsieur, will you please ask your mother if she knows anything about the Comte d'Estoban's grand-son? Being a servant in the Arblong household I know how devoted she will be to the family, and there is just a chance that the poor boy escaped and is still alive.'

'But certainly I ask Maman nex' letter I send to 'er, Madame, but zese letters zey take many days to travel from England to France and zen to return again.'

'Oh I know, but if you will do that I shall at least feel that his friends are doing all they can to help the Comte to find his grand-child.' She opened her purse and took out a half-

108

sovereign and gave it to him. 'That is for your trouble, Monsieur.'

'Madame is all goodness.' He bowed and put the half-sovereign in his pocket and stood there behind his stall jingling the money in his pocket and staring at Melissa in a way that made her thankful to drag her aunt away.

Sophy had finished with the musical boxes and Mr. Beaumont was carrying her purchases for her, and from the expression on his face as he listened to her chatter it was plain that he had put Melissa and her tiresome aunt from his mind.

After Sophy had driven off in Mr. Beaumont's chaise, smiling her thanks to the young officers, Melissa and Miss Cheriton followed them down the hill in a hired chaise, the horse's hoofs slipping on the cobbles, the harness jingling in a way that found no answering gaiety in Melissa's heart.

'It is no good being cross with me, Mel,' said her aunt as they went. 'I was determined to do what I could for our dear old émigré and I have done it, and why you thought that Fouquet man to be so dreadful I cannot imagine. He was most polite – foreign of course – but *very* polite.'

'The Comte would hate to have his affairs talked about though, Aunt Charity,' said Melissa reproachfully. 'You know how terribly proud he is.' She remembered how, three years earlier, when she was at Tamporley, she had tried to express the sympathy of her sixteen-year-old heart, to be met by an icily polite: 'But one does not show one's emotions in public, my dear Miss Melissa,' that had the effect of stopping her in mid-stream, and dried up the gushing words as if a tap had been turned off.

So would the Comte's friends have behaved as they were summoned from the prison for the guillotine, with a final tap of their fingers on the lids of their snuff-boxes, a smiling bow, a cool dignity, and an apology for being unable to finish a game of cards . . . She could guess how angry the old man would be if he knew how his affairs had been discussed by Miss Cheriton with a common prisoner in the Castle prison.

'But my dear child, the whole town knows about M. Estoban's grand-son,' protested Miss Cheriton, uneasily conscious now that her niece might be right. 'That old servant of his has never stopped talking about him ever since they arrived in Tamporley.'

'But we have never heard the Comte mention him.

'Of course not, dear. Wild horses would not make him . . . But that need not seal our lips too. I have no doubt that Monsieur Fouquet's mother is a thoroughly nice woman and, like so many of these old retainers, devoted still to the Arblongs and the Estobans. I would not be at all surprised if we were to learn something in her next letter to her son.'

Melissa argued no more: her mind went back to the smile on Edward Beaumont's face as Captain Woodcock had helped Sophy to mount to the seat beside him in his chaise, and it was a subject even more depressing to contemplate than the fate of the Comte's lost grand-son.

*       *       *

Up at the Castle Fouquet was packing his toys away when Gaston came.

'You have done a good trade this morning?' asked Lecointre.

Fouquet shrugged. 'Enough,' he said. After a moment he added, 'You remember that old man who came to pay the Lieutenant's money to us that day as if we were his lackeys?'

'The old Frenchman who was with the Agent, do you mean?'

'Who else? I have learned today that he is one of these sacrés émigrés. Did you know that?'

'What of it?' Gaston was not interested.

'Who told you then?' demanded Fouquet.

'One of the laundry-maids at the hospital when I was doing some work there. She is a great gossip that one, and she likes to tell everybody about this old émigré.' Gaston spread his hands. 'One would think he was the only one in England.'

'Perhaps you remember the ring on his hand there? . . . It is

110

common knowledge that these émigrés took all their money and jewels with them when they left France. That diamond in this old man's ring must be worth a fortune!'

Gaston shrugged. 'I don't see that it matters to us.'

'But then you see nothing, my dear Gaston. Your mind was born blind, like a kitten. Did your obliging laundrymaid tell you where the old man lives, parbleu?'

'I think she said he was at Tamporley, but I cannot be sure. I do not speak English well, as you know, and I may not have understood her. But she talks of him all the time and so it is impossible not to understand something of what she says.'

'Tamporley? And where is that, for example?'

'It is a village on the hill on the far side of the town. You can see it from the South Gate on market days when the outer gates are not closed. The church has a pointed spire sticking up among the trees.'

'A good landmark that,' commented Fouquet and Gaston glanced at him curiously.

'What then is in your mind?' he wanted to know. 'Do you plan to seize one of the Castle cannon and fire upon this old émigré's house in Tamporley? You do not even know where it is situated . . . '

'But one can find out, no doubt,' said Fouquet with satisfaction. 'And having found out, I shall not forget. I am good at remembering things like that. I do not forget, for example, that my mother called me Arblon so that I should never forget that I was the child of a cursed aristo, and that I should never stop hating them as long as I lived.' He packed the little guillotine with care. 'I would be amusing to meet M'sieu le Comte d'Estoban one of these days . . . It would be amusing to see what he would say if I were to tell him, "M'sieu le Comte, I have taken a fancy to that ring of yours, and I have taken a fancy to that neck of yours, also. Before I snap it over my knee be so good as to tell me where your money is kept . . " It would be interesting to see if he remained so cold and aloof then . . . ' He laughed at Gaston's expression. 'My mother knew what she was about when she taught me to hate, my friend. Hate is a good tonic . . . it keeps a man alive.'

Then suddenly his expression changed and he caught his friend's arm. 'Who is that young man there, dismounting from his horse and handing it to the sentry to hold for him? Tell me then!'

Gaston's eyes followed his to the South Gate. 'Oh, that is only the surgeon from the town. He visits the hospital every day but poor Maugin is sick with a pain in his stomach, and so the surgeon has been sent for. He does not look best pleased either.'

'What time does he usually visit then?'

'Not until the evening. One says there is a young lady who lives not far from the prison here, and that he goes to visit her after he has seen his patients in our hospital.'

'He wears a good coat, that one, and a fine hat, and those gloves are fine ones too. No doubt he takes them off when he is seeing his patients in the hospital?'

'Oh yes. He leaves his gloves, hat and coat in the Superintendent's office downstairs and puts on an old coat that he keeps there for the purpose.'

'Good.' Fouquet smiled and went on packing his toys, but the next day he electrified his friend by asking if he could help with the nursing at the hospital.

As he was strong and could lift a man easily, and moreover had the fine, gentle hands of an artist, and because above all, they were short of nurses just then, his offer was immediately accepted.

# IO

As the days went by and the games of chess became more interesting and absorbing, the Comte found that he was not looking forward to his guest's departure, while as for old Jeanne, if the Lieutenant had been the intended occupant of the spare bedroom upstairs he could scarcely have been looked after better. For one thing she found it a change to have somebody to talk to in her own language.

'These English,' she grumbled. 'Never do they talk to you. Never! They say good-day and they smile in their grave fashion, but they are a sad, heavy race. No doubt it is the English weather. It cannot make a man cheerful to live continually in a fog.'

'There is one saving grace about the English weather, however,' said Philippe smiling. 'It seems to dismay the English as much as it does us. They never expect the snow, hail, rain and sleet that is unleashed upon them, although, ma foi, one would think they should envisage it by this time.'

'I do not like the English towns either,' went on Jeanne. 'Why do they have these pavements everywhere, when there is a road to walk on? In London some of our noble ladies showed their disapproval by walking in the roads and ignoring these pavements altogether.'

'That must have made them unpopular with the young gentlemen who like to drive their curricles at speed through the streets?'

'Undoubtedly it did, M'sieu, but who cares about them? In

Paris the young gentlemen of our nobility never made such an exhibition of themselves in the public streets. They would have been ashamed to do so. These English gentlemen behave like grooms and lackeys.'

'I remember how astonished I was by the straight rows of houses in the towns,' said Philippe. 'All exactly alike, with the steps up to the front door and the bow windows and the straight sashes above. It is droll, that.'

'And then there is the market,' went on Jeanne. 'They do not like it if I tell them that their goods are bad. In France I would say to the people who sold cabbages, "Look then," I would say, "this cabbage is bad. Do you expect me to pay good money for that? Find me another, if you please." And they would find me several to choose from at once. But here it is a matter of complete indifference to them, and they do not care who they cheat, and when I complain they look at me as if bad cabbages are good enough for the servant of an émigré.'

'But they do it to their own people as well,' the Lieutenant consoled her. 'For me the English Sunday is the worst of all.'

'Ah yes, you are right there.' Jeanne shrugged expressively. 'When we first came to England, Monsieur and Madame Henri d'Estoban and me, we cannot understand this English Sunday, with the silence in the streets, and no amusements, and no markets open . . . not even the baker's shop. It is sinister that, and the way the English march to church, as silent as if they walk in a funeral procession, with no conversation at all.'

But the English people who called upon the Lieutenant while he was staying with the Comte did not appear to lack conversation. At all times of the day English ladies, young and old, came to ask after the Romantic Frenchman's progress, and frequently they were joined by Edward Beaumont, who was on terms of intimacy now with Philippe, bringing with him some of the young officers from the militia regiments at the Castle.

M. Estoban enjoyed all this coming and going: the sound of

laughter and young voices in the house did his heart as much good as it did Jeanne's, and at the end of the fortnight he sent a note to Captain Buller requesting that the Lieutenant's leave could be extended by a further week, as the apothecary had not yet discontinued his visits. The Agent willingly agreed, and among the young ladies who were most outspoken in her delight was Miss Forsett, who told the Lieutenant that now he might accompany the Comte to the ball that was being given in the following week to celebrate her coming-of-age.

'And why should there be so much rejoicing that you have attained these years of discretion, Mademoiselle Sophy?' asked the Comte.

'I care nothing for years of discretion,' replied Sophy with a little laugh. 'But on that day I become an independent woman, Monsieur le Comte, with my fortune and my person entirely at my own disposal.

The Comte congratulated her gravely, but as he glanced at Philippe he noticed a look on the young man's face that made him uneasy. He remembered that he had often found them waiting for him in the salon when he came in from his morning drive, and that in his absence Philippe had been conversing in French with the young lady with only deaf old Jeanne for a chaperon. He couldn't help wondering if the affair had been quite as innocent as they would have him believe, and while he liked Philippe, and in fact found his liking for him growing as he came to know him better, he still could not quite bring himself to trust an officer in Bonaparte's army.

During the week before the ball he became more uneasy still, because it seemed that the Lieutenant had not only the heiress in mind when he set out to amuse himself. Chancing to look over the hedge one day as he walked in his little garden M. Estoban was disconcerted to observe a coat of a familiar shade of faded blue in the Tamporley woods, and the wearer of it was accompanied by a lady, a very little lady in a rose-coloured bonnet.

They were walking slowly together under the trees, deep

in conversation: her hand was on his arm and there was no doubt in the Comte's mind that the world was forgotten by at least one of them. And although the lady was married and in no need of a chaperon, on the following day M. Estoban thought that he too would take a walk in the Tamporley woods, and in a surprisingly short time he came upon Philippe Cadot and young Lady Tamporley, sitting together on a fallen tree-trunk in a little clearing to the right of the footpath.

March had borrowed a few hours from April that day, the sky was blue after a shower, and the sun was turning the budding leaves into a sparkling fairyland. The Comte was before them before they saw him, and he noticed that Philippe had the little lady's hand in his. He dropped it quickly as the émigré spoke and rose to his feet: there was surprise in his face but no guilt, and neither was there any of its usual laughter.

'I see that you are making the most of your last days at Tamporley, Lieutenant,' said M. Estoban pleasantly. 'And the weather is being kind to you also . . Lady Tamporley, your servant!'

The Lieutenant found himself firmly dismissed, and with a muttered excuse he bowed to her little ladyship and left them, striding back to the Comte's cottage with a frown on his handsome face.

The Comte saw that Lady Tamporley's pretty eyes looked heavy, as if she had shed tears not very long ago. He said gently, 'Is it permitted for an old man to take the young one's place beside you, Madame?'

'But of course.' But her welcoming smile quivered and her eyes were bright with moisture still. 'Sit down, Monsieur.'

'I thank you.' He sat down, fearful of the damp of the woods for his rheumatism, but spurred on by his deep affection for her.

'I never walk through these beautiful woods, Lady Tamporley,' he said gently, 'without being reminded of my daugh-

116

ter. She was small, like yourself, and fair, as you are . . . and she too loved the woods round my château at home.'

She glanced timidly at his face. 'Was . . . your château like Tamporley?' she asked.

'It was as large . . . and as beautiful.' The smile left his face as he thought of three carriages turning out of an avenue into roads choked with refugees, the woods they left behind desecrated by murder, the flowers trampled under foot, the château itself in flames . . . 'No matter. It is gone now.' He spoke abruptly and Sarah felt she could guess his thoughts.

'You must think me very fortunate, Monsieur,' she said.

The smile came back to his thin face. 'But of course you are fortunate, Lady Tamporley! These five charming children, not entirely separated from you by their so severe governess, this beautiful home, and' . . . he hesitated and then added, 'a husband who is not without merit.'

She looked at him quickly but she did not speak and after a moment he continued, 'Yesterday when I was out in my little chaise, driving through your charming country lanes, I came upon Sir Tamporley, leaning on a gate and studying a wide stretch of his land where it slopes down to the river and the water meadows. "Good morning, Sir Tamporley," I say, stopping my fat pony beside him. "Are you admiring your husbandry then?" He shook his head. "No, Monsoor," he says in that English way he has, "I am wondering if I shall not have a lake made down there this coming winter. It would be an easy matter to divert the stream into it." "A lake, Sir Tamporley?" I cried, astonished. "But why then do you want this lake?" He looked at me with that slow smile of his. "To give employment to a lot of poor labourers who will not otherwise find the money to feed their families," he said, as if charity on that scale was the most natural thing in the world. He then told me that several of his friends were doing the same on their estates, building new wings to their houses, excavating land drains, creating formal gardens, and erecting new stable blocks, not because they were necessary but to give employment to these poor men. "You see," he says, "at the rate Boney is losing his battles it looks as if the war may end any day now, and after that there will be short employment and the food prices will soar even higher than they are now." He threw back his head then and laughed, but I do not think that he found it a joke.' The old man paused. 'I was impressed by your husband, Lady Tamporley. I felt that I might have misjudged him.'

But what was a dull husband, however good, when weighed in the scales against romance? She was only twenty-six, and surely nobody could grudge her a short-lived hour on the hill-top to keep in her heart for ever? She thought of the smoke-blue eyes that had blazed down into hers, she thought of Philippe's handsome face and his deep, thrilling voice, not disguised by laughter and flowery compliments when he spoke to her alone, and she knew that the love that had come to her so suddenly had also come to him.

She could not think what the end of it would be and she did not care. The children were there in the background, but they were no longer part of her life. Even little James seemed to have grown apart from her in the last few days, and to be somebody else's child in a different world, just as Tamporley belonged now to a man who was no longer her husband. Some other woman would walk back to the house later on, to talk and act as young Lady Tamporley talked and acted, and she would take little James on her knee. But only a part of her would be there: the other part, the real part, the only part that mattered any more would be walking with Philippe and listening to his voice . .

A cloud came up to hide the sun and the world about them lost its sparkle. The Comte, seeing that her spirit had strayed a long way away from him got up and fussed a little, saying that the tree trunk was damp and it was going to rain.

'Yes,' she said. 'You must not sit here any longer.' She got up with him and gave him her hand. 'Thank you, Monsieur, for your kindness.'

With a heavy heart he kissed the hand held out to him and went away, but his manner was cool towards the Lieutenant that night and he did not play their usual game of chess. He said he was tired and he went early to bed, and as he lay there wide awake counting the slow hours, he found he was glad that only two days remained of Philippe's extra week, and that at the end of that time Tamporley would once more be out of bounds.

\*　　　\*　　　\*

The ugly house at Dove Tye was uglier than ever on the night of Sophy's ball, because the hundreds of candles that were burning seemed to accentuate the heavy furniture and the lack of taste in the rooms. The family portraits that frowned from the walls were of men with Squire Forsett's hawk-like nose and crimson complexion, the women had poor Sophy's pale eyes and stooping shoulders.

But that night at least Sophy was radiant, and having chosen her own dress she was clad more becomingly than her friends had ever seen her. The sea-green of the stripes in her silk dress matched the green of her eyes, and she was so happy that everyone who came in contact with her could not help catching a little of her happiness too, and told each other what a very nice girl she was. And it said a great deal for Sophy that very few in the ball-room that night remembered to be envious of her because she had come into a fortune that day.

Everyone was there, because the nights were moonlit just then, and among the guests were Captain Woodcock and some of his young ensigns, included with a last minute graciousness by Sophy's aunt. The Squire frowned on them when they arrived but as Edward Beaumont followed hard on their heels their intrusion was soon forgotten. Mr. Beaumont was looking quietly happy, and as Melissa watched him take his place beside Sophy to open the ball she heard Mrs. Forsett telling

119

the Dowager that his proposal could be considered as having been made.

'He will ask her tonight, in my opinion,' she declared.

The Dowager remarked that she had never seen Sophy look so well.

'Mr. Beaumont said the very same thing to me when he arrived,' said Sophy's aunt. 'He is very much in love with her, of course.'

Melissa tried to move away but her movement was noted and she was pounced upon.

'What, Miss Melissa, have you no partner? This will never do! Never mind, I can see Captain Woodcock over there – he will do for you very well. I will beckon to him . . . Oh, he has seen us and is coming over . . . I don't suppose you see many balls like this at home, do you, my dear?'

Melissa looked at the ugly room and Mrs. Forsett's hideous turban and said with truth that she did not.

'You have been away from home several weeks,' went on Mrs. Forsett. 'Do you expect to stay much longer in the neighbourhood?'

Melissa said it would depend on how long her Aunt Charity wanted her to stay.

'But who looks after your father while you are away? . . . Oh the Rector has a sister, has he? . . . And have you any servants? Three? That is rather a large number for a country rectory, isn't it? Your father's stipend cannot be very large. Has he any private money?'

Fortunately at that moment Frank Woodcock reached them and as she got up thankfully Melissa said that in another moment she would have torn the turban from Mrs. Forsett's head and stamped on it. 'I have never known anybody who aroused my temper more easily than she does,' she added. 'Poor Sophy! How glad she will be when tonight is over!'

'What do you mean?' He looked at her so sharply that she was surprised.

'But what should I mean other than that now she is her own mistress?' she asked.

'Oh . . . of course!' He looked a little confused. 'I had forgotten about the wretched fortune . . .'

'Then you should not forget it. You should treat it with respect, because I am sure it is the only thing about Sophy that her father and Mrs. Forsett consider to be important.

'I daresay you are right.' But he was looking across the room to where Sophy was dancing with Edward Beaumont, and at the same moment they saw him and a smile passed between the three of them, and once more Melissa felt that there was some secret that they all shared and in which she had no part.

'There's something between you and Mr. Beaumont and Sophy,' she said peevishly. 'I wish you would tell me what it is.'

'I'm afraid I don't understand you.' But his slight flush and quick laugh gave him the lie, although she saw that he had not the least intention of telling her about it

'You used not to be secretive,' she complained.

'Ah, but then you were sixteen, Mel, and I was twenty,' he reminded her. 'But you are not the only one who scents a mystery here tonight. For the last few minutes I have been wondering where Cadot got his coat! It fits him so beautifully and it is of such handsome cloth that I am wondering if he has borrowed it from Beaumont for the occasion.'

'He may have done.' Melissa glanced at the handsome Frenchman without interest. 'It would be like Mr. Beaumont to have lent it to him. He is a very kind man.'

Frank glanced at her face. 'You knew him before he came here, didn't you?' he said.

'Slightly.' She spoke hurriedly. 'Mr. Cadot dances very well, doesn't he?'

'He points his toes too much!' He laughed. 'But I was never a good dancer myself, so I cannot criticise another's performance. I wonder how long it will be before young

Halstead can no longer stand on his feet? He was tipsy when he arrived and he has been drinking steadily ever since.'

'Oh dear!' Melissa glanced apprehensively at the flushed young man leaning up against the doorway into the supper-room for support. 'I hope he won't make a scene?'

'I should not think so.' The Captain spoke cheerfully. 'The best thing he can do will be to drink himself insensible as soon as possible.'

On the other side of the room the Lieutenant was dancing with Sarah. They did not speak much, and the Lieutenant's gay chatter had deserted him. He seemed to be concentrating on the steps of the dance, and his voice was so quiet that only she heard what he said.

'When I get back to the Castle tomorrow I am going to ask the Agent if I can move to lodgings in the town.'

'But I thought lodgings were too expensive for you?'

'They are. But I have a little money put by and it would be worth while to spend it in that way.'

'Do you know of good lodgings, Monsieur?'

'The name is Philippe, ma petite . . . '

'Hush . . . somebody might hear you . . . '

'There are some rooms, I understand, over a baker's shop. The landlady is very accommodating and does not mind if one has . . . visitors . . . ' His eyes met hers. 'Do you advise me to take them, Lady Tamporley?'

'You must do as you please.' Her eyes were shining with a happiness that was half-agonised as she was torn this way and that.

'We will talk of it again later,' he said, and they went down the dance together and parted. The room seemed to be full of curious faces, and Sarah, dreading what they might discover in her own, found herself next to the Comte.

'Lady Tamporley, you are looking pale,' he said, concerned. 'Will you not let me get you a glass of wine?'

'No thank you, Monsieur. But I can see an open window in the ante-room and a chair beside it. It will be better than

122

this hot room.' She put her hand on his arm and let him conduct her to the ante-room, where an astonishing sight met their eyes.

Young Mr. Halstead was sitting sprawled in a chair, an empty wine glass in his hand, and he was gazing up at Sarah's husband with a silly smile on his face. It was evident to anyone that he was very drunk indeed.

'I have told you that you have had enough, sir.' Tam was saying in a voice that he tried to keep to the level of discretion. 'Be a sensible fellow, and let me or Beaumont here take you home.'

'No, then, b'God I will not.' Young Halstead waved his glass at Tam. 'I'm not so drunk's all tha' and we aren't at Madame Genie's now m'dear fellow . . . You can't tell me wha' to do and neither c'n Beaumont, damn his eyes. You c'n both go t'hell!'

Tamporley, suddenly aware that he and Beaumont were not alone with the young man, glanced up to see his wife there with M. Estoban. He made a quick movement towards her but she retreated swiftly, and he heard her say to the old émigré that the ante-room seemed to be scarcely the place for ladies at the moment.

As they vanished from the room Tam descended furiously upon the young wastrel with the wine-glass. 'You young blackguard!' he cried. 'I'll thrash you for this, damn me if I won't . . . ' And then he felt his arm taken and held in a friendly grip.

'If you take one side of him, sir, and I take the other,' said Edward Beaumont gently, 'we can get him out by the other door and so to my carriage. My servants will drive him home and get him to bed before he knows what they're about. I'll warn them not to let him come back.' Then, seeing the angry uncertainty on Tam's face he added, 'It is the quickest way, I think, to avoid any more scenes.'

The baronet knew that he was right. Young Halstead always became abusive when he was drunk and he did not want the whole ball-room to know about his visit to Madame Genie's. So between them he and Edward Beaumont lifted the young man up and carted him off to the carriage and left him to Mr. Beaumont's servants to take home, and having seen him off the premises Sir Tamporley returned to the ball-room in search of his wife.

He found her sitting at the open window, in an ante-room that was now completely empty, as the next dance was in progress.

'My dear, you'll catch cold without something round your shoulders.' He came to her quickly and saw her look up at him in surprise at his sudden concern for her.

'Thank you, but the night air is refreshing,' she said.

He sat down beside her.

'Look here, Sarah,' he said quickly, 'that young Halstead was drunk . . . '

'Oh yes, Tam,' she agreed mildly. '*Very* drunk I'm afraid.'

'There was absolutely no truth in what he said,' he told her, and then as she did not seem to understand he ploughed on honestly, because he was a very honest man, 'At least, I did go to Madame Genie's once . . . '

She was singularly undismayed and not at all shocked. 'Yes, Mamma told me you had been there,' she said.

His jaw dropped. '*What?*' he exclaimed. 'Mrs. Forsett told you . . . ? How the devil did she know?'

'I never know how Mamma finds out about such things,' said Sarah equably, and incredibly she smiled.

'But you never said anything about it to me!' His voice was outraged and rising in wrath: in fact, it was so evident that she was the one who had been in the wrong that she felt compelled to defend herself.

'Why should I?' she protested gently. 'It was your business after all.'

'But . . . ' His sense of injury deepened. 'Didn't you . . . mind?'

Her eyes met his directly and he noticed that her smile

had disappeared. 'Would it have mattered to you if I had minded?'

He did not reply. He felt affronted and hurt by her attitude but he did not know what to say. It had never been easy for Tam to express his inmost feelings. 'I went to that harpie's house to fetch out young Halstead,' he said heavily. 'His mother asked me to go . . . She did not want his father to discover that he was there.'

He did not know if she had heard him, or understood what he had said. She seemed to have moved away from him although she was so near that he could have traced the embroidered flowers on her gown with the tip of his finger.

'That is a new dress, I think,' he said. 'What are those little gold flowers?'

'Fleur de lys.' But she seemed to be farther away from him still. 'The lily of France.'

'Briggs's smuggler brought it, I suppose?' He tried to laugh about it. 'A wiser man would have had his silk embroidered with roses.'

'But French lilies are more charming than English roses,' she said quietly, and turned towards the door where a man had appeared, looking for her. 'I am here, M. Cadot,' she said.

But even as he came to claim her for the next dance he was forestalled.

'I am sure the Lieutenant will forgive me, Lady Tamporley,' said M. Estoban smoothly, 'if I claim the prerogative of age. This dance is to be a quadrille I believe, and I would like to see, with your assistance, if a quadrille in England is mastered as easily as it was in France.'

She could not refuse him, but she dropped her fan as they passed the Lieutenant and he picked it up and gave it to her, their fingers touching for a fleeting moment.

'Fleur de lys indeed!' said Tam in disgust.

'I beg your pardon, Monsieur?' said the Lieutenant from the doorway. 'You spoke to me?'

'I did not.' Across the empty room the eyes of the two men met and for a second hatred flickered between them, and then Tam, who refused to create a scene in a house where he was a guest, stepped out on to the terrace to cool his temper and his head.

# II

A few days before Philippe was to return to the Castle the prisoner Fouquet signalled to his friend Lecointre as he made his way past the hospital block to the officers' rooms in the Keep.

'What do you want?' Gaston stopped a moment, aware of the sentry's eyes upon him. Conversations between prisoners from different sides of the Castle were not encouraged.

'A pair of boots,' said Fouquet easily.

'A pair of boots?' Gaston was astonished. 'What do you want boots for in the hospital? And what makes you think that I can provide you with them in any case?'

'I want the boots for wearing outside the hospital, imbecile,' growled Fouquet. 'And you are the only person I know who can get me a pair. Lieutenant Cadot has two pairs hasn't he?'

'He has the new pair that he was wearing when he left the Castle, and there is an old pair in his rooms that he keeps for when the others have to be repaired.'

'The old ones will do. And I want a piece of soap.'

'Soap?' Gaston's voice grew shrill. 'You know quite well that soap is rarer than gold in this place . . . Where am I to find such a thing? Tell me that if you please!'

'Where you find the boots of course. Where else?'

'But directly the Lieutenant returns he will discover that he has been robbed and he will dismiss me . . . Sacré! First his boots and then his soap! It is not possible.'

'Keep your voice low. That sentry is too interested in what

127

we are saying . . . I'm not asking you to steal anything. I only want to borrow the boots for the space of a day or two. That I promise you! And when have you known me to break a promise?'

'Often,' said Gaston sorrowfully. A silence fell between them and then Lecointre said resignedly, 'You have another plan for escaping, I suppose?'

'Yes, and I have no objection to telling you what it is.' His friend grinned unpleasantly. 'Listen, my dear, this old émigré who called at the Agent's office that day – he is my grand-father.'

'You astonish me!' Gaston was sarcastic. 'And in return let me tell you something. Captain Buller is my father! So now we have surprised each other.'

Fouquet scowled. 'You may laugh,' he said, 'but I have been talking to your friend the laundry-maid in the hospital about this old émigré, and it seems that he lives alone with one woman servant in his house in Tamporley – it is the first house on the right-hand side as you enter the village. I was told also by the old English lady that all his family was exterminated during The Terror, except for one grand-son, and that it is his great desire to find this grand-son again. Voilà! Here is his grand-son!'

'You are talking about yourself?'

'Exactly. Did you not notice how interested he was in my name – Arblon? All I have to do is to get my foot inside the old man's door with my story of being his grand-son, and once I am in . . . ' He grinned and drew his finger across his throat.

The laughter died out of his friend's face. 'A joke is a joke, but this is going beyond it,' he said gravely. 'You may have escaped from prison many times but you have not reached France yet, and I see no reason why you should do any better this time. And remember this, my friend: prisoners who murder when they escape are hanged, like any civilian prisoner. It is the law of England.'

'Ah well, perhaps I will not kill the old man. I will just tie him up and help myself to his jewels and his money.'

'And where will his servant be all this time? Will she assist you, for example?'

'I shall think of some way to entice her outside and dispose of her first. It should not be difficult.'

'I hope it won't be difficult, but I have my doubts. The older the hen the louder she cackles, and first of all you have to get yourself out of the Castle remember.'

'That presents no difficulty at all, where I am situated now. The young doctor leaves his brown cloth coat, his tall beaver hat, his gloves and his riding crop downstairs in the Superintendent's office. The Superintendent provides him with this old coat, as you say, and he puts it on and makes the rounds of the hospital as quickly as he can, anxious to be done with the business and on his way to see his mistress. But his examinations and his diagnosis do not matter to you and me: what does matter is that you must be ready with the Lieutenant's boots on the night after he gets back here, because it is then that we shall know the émigré is alone with the servant at Tamporley. The boots you will leave beside the surgeon's coat in the office, the soap in the meantime I will have given to a patient upstairs who has promised for a consideration to put it in his mouth and give an excellent imitation of a fit directly the doctor arrives at his room. That will be my opportunity. I am trusting to the soap to delay him long enough for me to able to get downstairs and into the coat, hat, boots and gloves, so that I may mount the horse that is always tied up near the sentry outside the South Gate and ride off, saluting the sentries with my riding crop as I go. It will be moonlight and excellent for finding my way, but that gateway is always deep in shadow and the sight of the doctor's clothes should be enough for them at the gate. I hope I shall not be challenged.' He watched the other's face. 'I see that even you are impressed by the simplicity of the affair.'

'It is too simple. And overlooking the matter of the soap

which must be stolen from the Lieutenant's room, what is going to happen to his boots? Will you abandon them when you abandon the surgeon's horse?'

'Exactly. I will lay them across the saddle . . . '

'So that anybody may steal them. That is a fine idea certainly. Those boots may be old but they were made by one of the best boot-makers in the town. They cost the Lieutenant a great deal of money.'

'Then I will leave them in the old émigré's house. How will that please you? Mon dieu! I never knew anyone so difficult to satisfy! The Lieutenant was staying there, wasn't he? Very well. People will say that he left them behind when he left, and he will not be implicated in my escape and neither will you.'

Gaston felt there was some grave discrepancy in this argument if he could but find it. Would the Lieutenant, for example, be so crazy as to leave behind such a precious possession as a pair of boots, however old they might be? But if Fouquet had set his mind on doing this thing it was best to humour him.

After all he had not been on a horse for years, and the animal would be quite likely to throw him off long before he got past the sentries at the South Gate. In which case the Lieutenant's boots would be safe . . .

*    *    *

The Agent received the Lieutenant's request to seek lodgings in the town with kindness, glancing at the young man's face with concern. Certainly the murderous attack on him had not done him any good. 'Can you afford such lodgings?' he asked.

'For a few weeks.' Philippe felt that he could not face the prospect of being incarcerated in the Castle again with only a daily promenade round the town for diversion and exercise. There was a baker in Market Street, he added, whose wife let lodgings to French officers and she was willing to take him. He had called there on his way this morning and the room she had vacant looked comfortable enough and it was said that she was an excellent cook. He did not add that the window of the room looked on the street by which the carriages entered the town from Tamporley.

'Very well.' Captain Buller thought that good cooking was probably what the Lieutenant needed most at the moment. 'Don't forget though that your parole area is still the same, and that although you need not be indoors by curfew you will have to report to me here once a week.'

'I understand, Captain Buller. And I thank you very much.' And Philippe went away to find Gaston to tell him to pack his clothes.

This unexpected turn of events filled the good Lecointre with dismay. He managed to filch a piece of soap from the Lieutenant's belongings, but the boots were a different matter. When he met Fouquet on his way to the hospital that morning he gave him the soap and told him that he must do without the boots.

'But I must have them!' Fouquet refused to see reason in any matter that affected himself. 'Tell him they must be mended. Has he not his best pair to wear?'

'I will see what I can do,' said Lecointre doubtfully.

'I should think so indeed,' scowled Fouquet. 'I am depending on you, and the boots must be left downstairs with the other things tonight. The moon is already on the wane, and I cannot find the émigré's house in the dark.'

Gaston went back to the Lieutenant and begged him to allow him to take his old boots to the prison mender.

'They are not worth it,' said Philippe indifferently.

'But Lieutenant, they are in holes, and when they are mended you will be able to wear them for months, possibly for another year. If you will consent to wear the new boots today I will have the old ones mended and at your lodgings by tomorrow morning. I know the baker's wife and I will give them to her when she calls at the market: you will have them when she brings you your rolls and chocolate.'

131

It hurt him to deceive the good Lieutenant with such a load of lies, but Fouquet was in an ugly mood and Gaston had no wish to be in hospital himself with a broken head.

Gaston's insistence on the repairing of the boots gave Philippe the impression that the mender was a friend of his and in need of work, and so he humoured him and spent the rest of the morning removing his belongings to the lodgings in Market Street. Gaston went off quickly with the old boots before he could change his mind, and left them wrapped in a bundle of dirty linen in the hospital laundry until it was time to slip them into the Superintendent's office with the surgeon's outdoor clothes.

That night things went with almost too great an ease. The surgeon came upstairs as usual, clad in the old coat, and made his rounds with the Superintendent even more speedily than before, glancing at the patients with only a cursory interest and evidently impatient to get away. Fouquet caught the eye of the man who had promised to simulate the fit with the help of the soap and a reward of three shillings, and slipped away down the stairs. He went for the boots first and was chagrined to find that they were too small for him, but the leather was thin and as he forced them on they split up the back.

But it was not likely, he thought, that the sentries would glance at the back of his legs. The coat and hat and the general appearance of the doctor was all that was wanted, and he took heart, remembering the occasion when he had been acting in a play that had required an English soldier, and he had borrowed the uniform of one of the Ensigns for the performance and walked out of the prison in it, with the sentries saluting him right and left. It is true that he had been captured after a few days, but there was no other chance of escaping from the Castle except in disguise. Tunnelling under six to ten foot walls with the chance of coming up under the moat was certainly out of the question.

Dressed in the surgeon's coat, hat and gloves, and carrying his riding crop in his hand, he strode out of the hospital

132

in his split boots and walked boldly down to the South Gate, and here again luck was with him, because the turnkey was having an argument with the sentries on duty and none of them gave him more than a glance as he untied the horse and swung himself up on the animal's back. In a surprisingly few minutes he was outside the Castle walls and riding young Maple's horse down the road in the direction of the village on the opposite hill.

As he came into open country and the moonlight showed him his surroundings more clearly his spirits rose: he touched the horse's sides with his heels and made him canter, and then stopped abruptly as he found it difficult to keep his seat. He had never been a good rider, and the horse, knowing him to be a stranger, did not take kindly to heavy hands on the rein nor to heels dug viciously into his belly. He started to move sideways, almost unseating his inexperienced rider, so that he cursed him roundly in his own language, the road being empty of travellers.

He reached the village at last however and stopped outside the first house on the right, pulling on the rein until the beast beneath him ceased its crab-like walk, and then he sat back, staring at the house with disgust and disbelief, his dreams of wealth and jewels filched from a rich émigré fading

It was a very small house, one might almost call it a cottage in fact, and through the downstairs window he could see the Comte sitting at a table, reading a book by the light of one candle. For a moment, so great was his disappointment. Fouquet hesitated, wondering if he would not go on while he had a horse under him to take him on his journey to the coast, and without wasting time and trouble on the émigré. Then he saw the old man raise his hand to turn a page and the great ring flashed in the candlelight.

Fouquet slid off the horse's back, tied it to the gate-post and slipped round to the back of the house. And as he arrived at the back door the Castle gun sounded, echoing round the

133

small English hills, to tell the neighbourhood that one of the prisoners had escaped.

\* \* \*

When the baker's wife brought his chocolate and rolls in the morning Philippe was not really surprised to find that she brought no boots with her.

'I knew they would not be ready, Madame,' he said.

'I daresay everybody was upset about the escape last night,' she said.

'Of course.' The chocolate smelt good and the rolls were hot from the oven, but she looked on with disapproval while he attacked them with an appetite.

'That's poor thin stuff to start the day on,' she told him. 'A draught of English beer and a cut of cold roast beef or hot mutton chops would do you much more good.'

'Nevertheless these are delicious.' He smiled at her reassuringly. 'Did you hear the prisoner's name when you were at the Castle this morning, Madame?'

'Well, I did hear it, but I don't know that I can remember it . . . Would it be Fookay, Mr. Cadot?'

Philippe laughed. 'It is very likely to be Fouquet, Madame. He is always escaping, that one. But they will bring him back. They always do.' He resigned himself to wearing his new boots until Gaston had got over the shock of his friend's departure.

It was market day in Doverton and for a time the Lieutenant amused himself by watching the people and the farmers' gigs making their way to the market. He knew there was no chance of seeing Sarah that day: the Dowager and her daughter-in-law avoided the town on market day, finding it too difficult to make a way through the herds of cattle and the flocks of sheep and the pigs and the geese that were driven along the lanes. At noon he thought he would go and call on Miss Cheriton and Melissa, hoping to hear something of young Lady

Tamporley from them. He had not seen her since the night of Sophy's ball, and the thirty hours or so that had intervened already seemed more like a week.

Melissa and her aunt were entertaining Mrs. Halstead and Mr. Edward Beaumont. The ladies were delighted to see him, asking at once for news of the escaped prisoner, the subject that was uppermost in everyone's mind that morning. Mr. Beaumont however appeared to be thinking of something else and only joined in the conversation with an effort.

When Philippe told them the escaped prisoner's name he saw a look of alarm spring into Melissa's eyes as she glanced at Mr. Beaumont.

'Not that horrible man!' she cried.

'He is not a nice character, Mademoiselle,' Philippe agreed, adding in surprise, 'But surely you don't know him?'

'We saw him at the Castle when I went to buy my workbox,' said Miss Cheriton. 'And although Mel didn't like him and everyone said how dreadful he was, I must say I did not think he was so bad. He is very clever at making those delightful little toys. Mel bought one for the Tamporley children.'

Melissa was about to ask Philippe if he had seen the toy guillotine that Fouquet had made when the door burst open and Patty ran in, followed bashfully by a young man whom they recognised as the stable boy Ted from the livery stables behind the Tamporley Arms.

'Oh, Miss!' she cried. 'Please, Miss, I brought Ted in to see you, because he's brought you some of those brown eggs that you like so much, from Mother, Miss, and he says that the escaped prisoner was at Tamporley last night, and he broke into the old French gentleman's house there, saying as he was his long-lost grand-son, or some such dreadful story, and he stole everything he had and nearly murdered him and old Jeanne into the bargain.'

'Oh dear!' Miss Cheriton sat down again rather suddenly.

'But how could Fouquet know anything about M. le Comte's grand-son?' demanded Philippe. 'He never went outside the

Castle walls . . . How could he have heard about it, or know where Monsieur lives?'

'Oh dear!' said Miss Cheriton again. She thanked Patty and the young man and told them in a faint voice that they might go, and when the door was shut behind them Melissa said grimly, 'You had better tell the Lieutenant what happened at the Castle market, Aunt Charity.'

'I am sure I meant it for the best,' moaned Miss Cheriton wringing her hands. 'He seemed such a nice man . . and with that name of Arblong which Jeanne told me herself was the name of the Comte's daughter-in-law . . . I only asked Mr. Fouquet to write to his mother and ask her if she knew what had happened to M. Estoban's grand-son . . . I thought if she were a devoted old servant to the Arblong family she might know something about him. But he didn't ask me where the Comte lived and I certainly didn't tell him, so it can't be my fault.' She broke off. 'He was such a kind man,' she reiterated helplessly.

'As kind as a wild beast waiting to get its teeth into its prey,' said Philippe shortly. 'Once the idea was put into his mind he would not find it difficult to discover where his quarry lived. There are plenty of gossips visiting the Castle every day.' He got up.

'Where are you going?' asked Mr. Beaumont.

'To see what has happened at Tamporley.'

'Then you must let me take you. My chaise is at the door.' Mr. Beaumont followed him, leaving Miss Cheriton in tears and Melissa searching for the smelling salts. Her search brought her into the hall and she said in a whisper to the two young men, 'You must not blame her too much. I did my best to stop her that day, but she was carried away by her desire to help the Comte. Poor Aunt Charity is much too romantic.'

Philippe smiled politely and bowed, anxious to be gone, but Edward Beaumont stopped a moment to glance down at her pretty, troubled face. 'Romance,' he said gently, 'can be a very good thing, Miss Melissa, when it is not misplaced.'

She thought she read a meaning in the words that made her flush miserably. Would he never forget, she wondered wretchedly, how misplaced his own romance had been in her hands? She said hastily that she must find the smelling salts and left him to join the Lieutenant in the chaise.

As they bowled up the road towards the village of Tamporley Philippe said, 'By the way, Edouard, this has put the other thing out of my mind . . . I hope the affair went smoothly last night?'

'I have had no opportunity yet of discovering if it did or not,' replied Mr. Beaumont with a smile. 'But as my cattle are considerably faster than those at Dove Tye I thought it wise to remove them this morning before the hue and cry is raised, in case they might be needed for pursuit.

'It looks then,' observed Philippe gravely, 'as if two people at least have found happiness . . .' He sighed, thinking of Sarah. 'It is not come by so easily as a rule, Edouard.'

'No, Philippe, it is not,' agreed Mr. Beaumont and sighed also, frowning at the horses' ears.

# 12

Old Jeanne opened the door to them, showing no signs of the night's adventure except for a piece of court plaster on her nose.

'Jeanne!' Philippe caught her hands. 'You are all right then? God be thanked for that! . . . And Monsieur le Comte?'

'He is also unharmed.' Jeanne glared at him wrathfully. 'But who told that monster? That is what I want to know . . . Who told this beast about M. le Comte's grand-son? And who told him where we lived, parbleu? Tell me that, Lieutenant, if you please!'

They told her about Miss Cheriton and her work-box, begging her to forgive the lady for her well-meant indiscretion, and the frown between her eyes faded as she listened.

'Miss Cheriton talks a great deal, that I know,' she conceded at last, the occasions when she herself had told the story of M. le Comte's grand-son to the world conveniently forgotten. 'She is a lady whose occasional silliness may be forgiven for her goodness of heart.'

'It was all most innocently done,' said Mr. Beaumont, adding his persuasions to his friend's. 'And with the best intentions. Poor Miss Cheriton is so romantic, Madame.'

Jeanne agreed with them again. 'The English have no idea when to talk and when to keep silent,' she said severely. 'When they should be gay they are as silent as the grave, and when they should keep silent they commit indiscretions with every word they utter.'

'But M. le Comte, Jeanne?' Philippe had no desire to enter into another long discussion about the habits of the English. 'You say he was unharmed . . . but did the fellow attack him then? We heard that he had been half murdered and robbed of everything . . .'

'But, my dear Philippe, you should not believe everything that you hear,' said a voice behind him and he turned quickly to see M. Estoban descending the stairs. The great diamond ring was still on his finger, his hair was curled and powdered, and in his hand was the lace-edged handkerchief. An aura of lavender water came with him, and he was urbanely smiling.

'M. le Comte!' cried Philippe, who could have picked him up and hugged him, lace-edged handkerchief and all, in his delight. 'You are not hurt . . . That is all I want to know!'

'Did the fellow manage to break in?' asked Edward Beaumont, showing his own pleasure in the émigré's safety by his slow smile. M. Estoban led the way into the salon and told Jeanne to bring wine.

'It was she who was attacked, not I, Messieurs,' he said. 'The miscreant got his foot inside the back door and knocked her on the head. Fortunately her cap is a thick one and she wears her hair in a coil beneath it. She fell because she lost her balance, and directly he burst in here she got herself up and took to her heels, running down the road to the Tamporley Arms to fetch help. In the meantime I was seated over here, at this table, with my book.' He pulled open a drawer in the far side of the table, revealing a pair of duelling pistols in a case. 'I had sufficient warning to open this drawer and to remove one of the pistols before he entered, so that when he started demanding my money or my life I was able to reply that unfortunately it was his life that was in question, not mine. "These, Monsieur," I told him, "are duelling pistols. I have never been known to miss at ten paces and we are less than two apart." He saw the sense in my reasoning and took himself off.'

'So you let him go?' said Mr. Beaumont sorrowfully.

The old émigré smiled. 'He was my enemy,' he said. 'but he was also my countryman. One has to think of these things. And I have reason to believe that he will not be at liberty for long. The coat and hat that he was wearing were very distinctive.'

He put the pistol back in its case beside its fellow. 'I think I should keep these loaded,' he remarked. 'If the gentleman who called on me last night had realised they were empty he might not have been so open to argument.'

The young men laughed and after they had finished their wine Mr. Beaumont said he thought he should be going. 'I have some business in the town to enquire about,' he told them, and he went away leaving the Comte to gaze upon Philippe with all his old affection. 'My dear young friend,' he said, 'I have missed our game of chess sadly.'

'Then let us have a game now,' said Philippe gaily, and he took the board and the box of ivory chessmen from their place in the cabinet and set them out on the table.

Half an hour later however his host stopped in the middle of a move to regard him with consternation.

'I had forgotten,' he cried. 'You are back at the prison now and Tamporley is outside the parole area . . . Or is it different when you are in lodgings?'

'No, Monsieur. It is exactly the same as when I was at the Castle.'

'Then you have broken your parole in coming to see me!' The Comte shook his head reproachfully. 'Ah, Philippe, my dear boy, when will you learn that nothing must interfere with a gentleman's word of honour?'

'But, Monsieur, I had to know that you were safe.'

'It was not right. Honour is above all things, and when one has given one's word one does not break it, for any consideration whatever. That is why I still owe allegiance to the King of France.'

'But, Monsieur, a man's honour surely is his own concern, a thing for his own conscience. Something that might be a matter of consequence to M. le Comte d'Estoban is of no importance at all to Lieutenant Philippe Cadot in the Emperor's army.'

'Monsieur, you are treating with levity a most sacred subject!' The Comte pushed aside the chessboard angrily and the chessmen were swept to the floor.

Philippe stooped to pick them up. 'I beg your pardon, M. le Comte . . . You will not finish the game then?'

'No, I will not. You will oblige me by leaving my house at once, Lieutenant Cadot. I am seriously displeased with you.'

'Please receive all my apologies!' But there was the suspicion of a smile lurking about the Lieutenant's mouth as the last chessman was put back in the box, and M. Estoban saw it. He got up and went to the window and turned his back, and as Philippe's eyes rested on the outraged little figure they held an expression that was at once humorous and tender. 'When shall I visit you again?' he asked.

'You will *not* visit me again, Monsieur,' said the Comte frigidly, and then he added, 'I will visit your lodgings and take a glass of wine with you one day. But I am not promising that it will be tomorrow or the next day, Monsieur.'

'No, M. le Comte. But I will wait for you tomorrow morning in case you should come.' As he turned to the door however, he was called back.

'Philippe, my dear boy,' the Comte said gently, 'I miss your company greatly, and it will be a great pleasure to me to see you and to talk to you, but not at the price of your honour. Promise me then that you will not break your word again by visiting me here?'

'Very well, I promise.' And then, smilingly, he was about to leave when Jeanne appeared in the room with an old pair of boots in her hand: they were slit down the back.

'Do these belong to you, M'sieu?' she asked Philippe. 'I found them in the hedge by the back door.'

'If they are mine they should have my name in them.' Philippe took them from her and found his name marked plain. 'Now I see why Gaston was so anxious to have them repaired!' he exclaimed. 'They were for Fouquet!' He looked at the boots with disgust. 'They are certainly past repair now, in any case. Take them, Jeanne, and give them to the next beggar that comes this way with my compliments! I must manage with one pair.' He handed them back to her with a bow, bowed to the Comte, and went on his way.

The old émigré watched him from the window until he was out of sight and then he turned back to his empty salon with a sigh. The sunshine was fitful that morning, the wind chill. He huddled over his fire, holding out his delicate, blue-veined hands to the feeble flame.

'You love that young man,' Jeanne accused him.

'I have indeed become deeply attached to him.' He smiled sadly, glancing at the split boots in her hand. 'Don't throw those away just yet though, Jeanne. When I go to Doverton tomorrow to visit the Lieutenant I will take them with me to the bootmaker that Sir Tamporley patronises there, and I will have another pair made for him. It is quite scandalous,' he added with a dignified wave of his scented handkerchief, 'that an officer in the French army should only have one pair of boots . . .'

\*　　　\*　　　\*

The Lieutenant was strolling back to the town, his thoughts occupied with M. Estoban and the interrupted game of chess, and the wide gulf there was still between the old man's notions of honour and his own. It occurred to him that if the day ever came when the émigré returned to France he might find many of his old values swept away with his titles and his lands, and he wondered how he would respond to such a situation. That he would meet it with courage he did not doubt: pride would forbid such a man from admitting defeat, although every nerve in him might cry out against it.

The milestone that set the boundary was only a few yards

ahead of him when the Lieutenant heard rapid footsteps behind him, and a shadow fell across him, so that he wheeled quickly remembering vividly the moment of attack on the Heath, his senses alert for danger and on the defensive this time. And then he stood still and waited as he recognised in the man that hailed him Mr. Taylor's evil-looking apprentice, Josiah Hicks.

'I thought it was you!' The man caught up with him with a grin and put his hand familiarly on his arm. 'A Frenchy officer and beyond your boundary too. You ain't allowed a step this side of that stone there and well you knows it. Been to see your fancy piece, I dessay. Well, you can come along back to the Castle with me and we'll see what the Agent has to say to you.'

'To you, don't you mean, Monsieur?' Philippe smiled mirthlessly. 'It is the reward that you wish to receive no doubt. Alors, I will give you the ten shillings and you may go your way and leave me to go mine.'

'Oh no, you don't!' The apprentice's grasp tightened on his arm. 'You move a step wi'out me and I'll call for help. I'll fetch them labourers from that field yonder to help me hold you...'

'But if you do that they will want some of the reward of a certainty,' Philippe pointed out smoothly. 'So supposing you take your hands off me and allow me to walk in peace beside you to the Castle. Captain Buller is an excellent friend of mine, and it will be better if he hears of my crime from my own lips, I think.'

Josiah gave in with an ill-grace and they walked on together towards the town, and Philippe was strangely silent as they went, being aware of the odd feeling of danger that he had experienced when the shadow of the ungainly man had fallen across his own. Could it be possible, he wondered, that this was the man who had attacked him for that thirty pounds? When enquiries about the attack had been made nobody would have thought to mention seeing Mr. Taylor's apprentice on that lonely road that night: it was perfectly natural for him to have been there, on business for his master.

He tried to think of something that would fix the attacker in his mind. He had come on him from behind, and at one time his hat had fallen off . . . It was a beaver hat, like the one Josiah was wearing now . . . a very ordinary hat . . And yet was it so ordinary inside? . . . He remembered, quite suddenly, seeing a dark stain, shaped like a strawberry, in the crown . . . The light had not been good at the time, it is true, but the hat had fallen off beside him on the ground, and the stain was a dark one and showed up in the half-light. Again he looked at the hat and he smiled a little, wondering if Josiah had been delivered into his hands, and as the apprentice caught this smile and the glance the Lieutenant gave his hat, he looked slightly uneasy as if he wished he had left him alone and allowed somebody else to claim the money for his capture.

Presently as a clock down in the town chimed the hour he said he had no idea it was so late and he did not think he had time to go all the way to the Castle that day.

'I'll let you off this time, Frenchy,' he said with his unpleasant grin. 'You may think yourself lucky.'

'Oh, but I do think myself lucky, I assure you,' said Philippe smiling. 'And you cannot let me go once you have apprehended me. There are rules and regulations about these things.' His smile deepened as he saw Mr. Hicks's uneasiness growing. 'Let us press on together and see the Agent as soon as we can.'

In silence they went on down the road until they came to Doverton, and made their way through the streets turning up into Castle Street and so on to the Castle itself.

The sentries at the door in front of the Agent's house scarcely looked up as they arrived at the gate, and they did not cease their conversation with a young soldier who had just arrived from a neighbouring barracks. His uniform was splattered with mud as if he had ridden over rough country and his sweating horse was being rubbed down by a prisoner inside the Castle gates.

'Have you any notion what the despatch was about?' one of the sentries was asking as they arrived.

'That I haven't. I was told to ride hell for leather and give it into the Agent's own hands,' said the man. 'But I think it may well be the report of another victory.'

Philippe felt his heart sink. While a victorious Wellington might mean a quicker ending to the war he did not want to see his country beaten and the terms of surrender dictated by this English general and his allies. One of the sentries took them to the Agent's office and the militiaman at the door admitted them with a broad grin of welcome.

Captain Buller was at his desk with Colonel Delaney standing beside him, reading the despatch that had just come in. Both had been taking wine and appeared to be in excellent spirits.

Hicks, somewhat cowed now that he had his prisoner in front of the Agent, began to bluster and whine. 'Begging your pardon,' he said, twisting his hat in his hands, 'but I found this French officer at Tamporley village, walking along the road as bold as brass, which as you know, sir, is out of bounds to the likes of him . . . ' He broke off because the Agent was not listening.

'Well, Colonel Delaney?' Captain Buller said, smiling at the Colonel as he folded the despatch and returned it to him with a satisfied air. 'Does it mean the same to you as it does to me?'

'It does indeed,' said the Colonel. He lifted his glass. 'To the Field Marshal, God bless him!' he said.

'Amen to that.' The Captain turned on Hicks with an expression of distaste. 'Well? What is it about? What have you come here to say?' he demanded.

Once more Hicks started on his information, but he had got nowhere at all before he was again cut short.

'Tamporley *was* out of bounds to French officers,' Captain Buller told him. 'But it is so no longer. Lieutenant Cadot and his friends are free to go where they choose.'

'But . . . ' The apprentice stared, unable to take in the sense of this extraordinary pronouncement, and it had been lost on Philippe too. He had been staring at his captor's hat, and as it was turned this way and that in its owner's hands he saw the dark stain inside it, and it was the shape of a strawberry, and then he knew.

'So it was you who struck me down that night on the Heath and robbed me of my money!' he cried. 'I remember the stain in that hat . . . It fell off before you hit me the second time, remember?'

'You couldn't have seen me . . . ' Josiah stopped suddenly and the Agent, now extremely alert and interested, took him up quickly.

'Go on,' he said. 'Finish what you were going to say, Mr. Hicks . . . The Lieutenant couldn't have seen you because you were careful to keep behind him when you attacked him. That was it, wasn't it?'

'No, I didn't . . . it's a load of lies . . . ' Josiah made a bolt for the door and the militiaman there captured him quite easily.

'Take him to the guard-room,' commanded the Colonel. 'I'll hand him over to the constables presently . . . ' As Josiah was removed he came to Philippe and held out his hand. 'Allow me to be the first to shake hands with you, sir . . . My late enemy, and now, I hope, my friend.'

'Pardon, M. le Colonel?' Philippe wondered if he had gone mad. 'Forgive me, but I do not understand.'

'A despatch has just arrived from London.' The Agent got up from his desk and shook hands with him too. 'Boney has surrendered and the war is over. The fighting between our two countries has ceased. As I said just now, you are free to stay or to go where you like . . . even back to France.' He gripped the young Frenchman's shoulder kindly. 'And now I am going with the Colonel here to tell the good news to your fellow countrymen, and to set open the Castle gates.

He wrung the Lieutenant's hand again and left him there

146

alone, to make his way back to his lodgings scarcely knowing what he was doing or where he was going. As he reached the market he heard the cheering from the Castle: it followed him like the waves of the sea into Market Street and as far as the baker's shop. The baker's wife stopped serving her customers with her new-baked bread and turned to him.

'They are saying the war is over, Mr. Cadot, sir!' she cried. 'Perhaps you can tell us if it is true?'

'Yes,' he said. 'It is all over. We are no longer enemies, Madame.'

Immediately he found himself surrounded by men and women, shaking his hands, kissing him, embracing him, laughing and crying by turns. He freed himself with difficulty laughing because such behaviour was so foreign to the restrained, cold English, and then he went to the Creaking Gate and ordered the best dinner its genial hostess could provide, and when it was ready he sat down and ate it in company with what seemed to be half the officers at the Castle, both French and English.

When he had finished he walked on by himself to the Heath, and found a stretch of turf there and sat down, clasping his knees, and looked back at the town and the Castle on the hill with a queer feeling of regret.

He was free at last, and nothing could emphasise that more than the scent of the gorse flowers and the wild thyme that surrounded him. The lark that rose overhead was not more joyously free than he was at that moment, but somehow that joy, looked for and longed for over five years, was now overcast by sadness and regret.

He tried to think of his uncle, that bustling, kindly little man, and his aunt, neat and trim, with a mind given to housewifery and the management of money and the house. He tried to think of the house itself, and the vine that grew up the wall, his uncle's delight and constant care. He tried to think of the girls they had already selected for him to choose from for his wife, girls with nice little *dots* to bring him, and minds as full of

147

commonsense as his aunt's. Not one of them had a quiet gentle voice, golden hair like a halo, and the sweet face of an angel . . . Romance was too costly a commodity for himself, he realised that, and yet when he left England, he would leave behind something more rare and precious than he could ever hope to find again.

He sat there for a long time turning things over in his mind, and when night began to fall he strolled back to his lodgings through streets where yellow uniforms mingled happily with those of the militia. That night the ex-prisoners of war would return to the Castle to sleep because there was nowhere for them to go, but in a few days' time they would begin the journey to the coast and the boats that were to take them home.

He was making his way with difficulty through the throngs of merry-makers in the streets when he felt his arm seized for the second time that day and found Gaston beside him, rather drunk and very elated and above himself.

'So Lieutenant Cadot,' he cried. 'Here we are, brothers now, is it not? No longer master and servant – that is all past!' He glanced down at the Lieutenant's boots and burst out laughing. 'Fouquet has your old boots, but I daresay you guessed that. That was a good joke. The only time that Fouquet escapes successfully there is no longer any need for him to take all that trouble. When I heard the good news this morning I nearly died of laughing, thinking of him, you understand, hidden in ditches and behind hay-stacks and not knowing there was no need for such antics!'

Here, unwisely, he let go of the Lieutenant's arm and fell into the gutter, and Philippe left him there and went on to his lodgings.

But even there the fates had not finished with him that day, late as it was. A carriage was drawn up in a side street with a lady and gentleman in it, waiting for him, and as he reached the baker's shop the lady cried in a shrill voice, 'There he is! I'd know the rascal anywhere! . . . That's him without a doubt!'

'Arrest him, Smithson!' cried Squire Forsett, flinging himself out of the carriage, and a large man with a constable's truncheon in his hand seized Philippe by the collar.

'Is your name Philip Caddo?' he asked.

The Lieutenant wrenched himself free. 'I am Lieutenant Philippe Cadot of the French Army, Monsieur,' he said. 'And perhaps you will be so good as to tell me what you are doing and why you should lay your hands on me?'

The Squire answered him. 'You have eloped with my daughter, my man!' he shouted. 'That's what you've done, as if you did not know it for yourself! You drove off with her in a hired carriage last night and her aunt and I would like you to tell us at once where you have hidden her!'

'Hidden her? But why should I hide her, if you please?' Philippe stared at the Squire coldly. 'You are speaking about Mademoiselle Sophy I presume?'

'You know who he is talking about!' cried the lady, while the Squire shook his fist in the Frenchman's face and said threateningly, 'You need not think you are going to wriggle your way out of this. The war may be over, but we have law and order in England still, as you will see when you come up in front of the justices of the peace in the morning!'

'But on what charge, Monsieur?' Philippe sounded pained, although his eyes were dancing.

'On a charge of abduction, sir!' cried the outraged Squire. 'Take him away to the lock-up, Smithson. I will deal with him tomorrow.' And then he got back into the carriage beside his sister-in-law and was driven swiftly away.

Philippe accompanied the burly Smithson to the local lock-up with a shrug of his shoulders. These English were so pig-headed: Beaumont had been right there.

'*I* cannot do it,' he had pointed out. 'But if you, a Frenchman, were to do it nothing would persuade the Squire that you were not the villain of the piece.'

'I am charmed by your good opinion of me,' Philippe had protested. 'But a night in Doverton lock-up does not really

149

appeal to me. I prefer lodgings, if I am to be housed outside the Castle.'

'But my dear Philippe, it will give these two excellent young people time to get away,' Edward had insisted, and Sophy had added her persuasion to his.

'All you have to do is to take the carriage in your name,' she said. 'Dear Mr. Cadot, you are the kindest man – next to one – that I have ever met.'

Philippe sighed and accepted his fate. He was always ready to oblige a lady, and the plot they had hatched together had added a spice to life in the little town. One had to suffer, he supposed, for one's friends, but he was very much afraid the lock-up would be lousy.

# 13

Directly she heard that Doverton was thronged with French and English troops from the Castle the Dowager, fearful lest her sister's house should be broken into by drunken revellers, sent her carriage to remove Miss Cheriton and Melissa and the little maid Patty to the Dower House until the mood of the town had quietened.

Melissa enjoyed her two days' imprisonment at the Dower House, especially as Sarah shared most of it with her, although her cousin's wife seemed quieter than usual these days. In fact her gentle face showed no excitement when Tam joined them on the second morning of Melissa's visit with the news that Sophy Forsett had bolted.

'Bolted?' The Dowager stared, while Melissa, who was helping Sarah to wind silks, stopped with a strand of silk in mid-air. 'Do you mean that she has eloped, Tam?'

'Just so. She has eloped.' Tam was in high good humour: he disliked Squire Forsett immensely. 'And what is more, that old fool of a father of hers was so positive that she had eloped with one of the Frenchmen from the Castle that he had the fellow arrested and incarcerated in the local gaol. It was the man you liked so much, Aunt Charity . . . can't think of his name'

'You cannot mean dear Lieutenant Cadot, Tam?' Miss Cheriton was shocked, and Sarah dropped the spool of silk and slipped down on her hands and knees to look for it.

'But that is ridiculous!' cried the Dowager. 'Sophy would not elope with a Frenchman, dear! She is much too sensible!'

'That is what I told him,' said Tam. 'But he would have it that he used to meet her at the Comte's house, and in my park of all places!' He sounded indignant. 'If he did meet a girl in my park, and I wouldn't put it past him, mind you, it was much more likely to be one of the village lasses!'

'I don't believe a word of it!' said the Dowager. 'The spool, Sarah, my love, is just by your foot . . . '

'What I asked the Squire was this,' said Tam. 'If the man was supposed to have eloped with Sophy, why the devil didn't he go with her? Why is he still in Doverton?'

'What do you mean, Tam?' asked Melissa, interested.

'Why, on the night that Cadot was supposed to be with Sophy he was in the lodgings that he had taken only that morning in the town, and the baker who lets the lodgings and his wife are prepared to swear that he never left them all night.'

Sarah handed the silk back to Melissa and took up the spool again to continue their winding. 'Why did my uncle think then that it was Mr. Cadot who had run off with Sophy?' she asked.

'Oh, the carriage was ordered in his name,' said her husband carelessly.

'Mr. Cadot ordered Sophy's carriage?' Miss Cheriton was scarcely able to believe such a thing of her favourite. 'That plain girl!'

'Never mind about her looks,' said Tam. 'It seems that your Romantic Frenchman *did* order a carriage for Sophy, Aunt Charity, and that it did pick her up at the cross-roads beyond Dove Tye at ten o'clock that night. They have questioned the man at the livery stables and he swears it was Cadot who engaged him. But he did not go with Sophy. She travelled alone as far as Salisbury, where places had been booked for her and a gentleman on the night mail to London.'

The Dowager was placidly perplexed. 'And what does Mr. Cadot say about it, dear?' she asked.

'Oh, he denies that he had anything to do with it, beyond engaging the carriage for Sophy at her own request, and although I don't like the fellow he seems to be telling the truth.

Squire Forsett was going far beyond his rights when he clapped him in the lock-up, and I told him so. "The man is a French subject," I said, "and the war is over. Nobody has any right to keep a French officer locked up for an hour, let alone twelve, on the word of a post-boy or a livery-man." He didn't like it much, I can tell you.'

'Poor Mr. Cadot!' mourned Miss Cheriton. 'What a way to treat him! Where is he now, Tam?'

'At the Comte's house in the village.'

Sarah dropped the spool again. 'I cannot think why I am so butter-fingered this morning, Mel!' she said. She was no longer pale though, and she was smiling.

'You wouldn't think to look at that little émigré of ours that he could show much authority,' went on Tam, picking up the spool for his wife because it had rolled directly to him. 'But when he heard about Cadot's arrest he got out his chaise and he drove over to see Squire Forsett and told him that unless Lieutenant Cadot were immediately released he would take it up with the French authorities in London and charge the Squire with false imprisonment. Halstead, who happened to be there, told me that he was so coldly furious, and so much on his dignity, that the Squire not only agreed to release Cadot at once but actually begged his pardon into the bargain.'

Sarah laughed. 'When M. Estoban is angry,' she remarked, 'he can be a most daunting little person!'

Her husband glanced at her with a frown. Ever since the night of Sophy's ball she had seemed to have acquired a composure that had been lacking when he married her. She no longer turned white when he shouted, but waited till he had done and then reminded him mildly that she was not deaf. He found such odd behaviour disconcerting and did not know what to make of it. It was as if the real Sarah had got lost in an autumn mist and he was groping his way after her, unable to make any headway because of the heaviness of his feet.

'What does Mr. Beaumont say to Sophy's elopement?' asked the Dowager, and Melissa, waiting painfully for his reply,

heard Tam say that directly he had heard about it the gentleman had left Dove Tye for London, without even waiting to
say goodbye to the Forsetts, and that Halstead said he had
never seen a man so upset over anything.

Melissa could understand it. To be encouraged and then
thrown over by two different girls in less than six months! She
did not see how even a man of Edward Beaumont's fine
temperament could bring himself to meet any of them again.

*     *     *

At the end of a week Melissa and her aunt Charity returned to
Doverton: except for the news of Sophy's elopement they had
heard nothing of what had been going on in the town. Indeed,
Doverton might have been across the Channel or in Scotland
for all they knew to the contrary. Garbled accounts had reached
them through the servants at the Dower House that the
Frenchies had been looting and the militia had difficulty in
keeping the peace, that the militia had been making too free
of the liquor in the town and the Frenchies had to keep the
peace, that Frenchies and militiamen were walking about like
brothers, arm-in-arm, and that Frenchies and militiamen were
fighting each other on every street corner.

It was a relief to dine with Colonel Delaney and his wife on
the night of their return and to hear from the Colonel himself
that almost every prisoner had gone.

'I saw the last of 'em marching away this morning,' he told
them with satisfaction. 'Everybody in the town was still going
mad about the fellows, giving them food to take with them to
eat on the way and bottles of wine to put in their knap-sacks. I
cannot think what has come over the English people.'

'Well, naturally they want to part friends, dear, said his
wife. 'And some of those poor men had been at the Castle for
more than ten years.'

Her husband laughed. 'One of them has not gone yet however,' he said. 'Your Romantic Frenchman, Miss Cheriton,

154

Philippe Cadot . . . But he is to go in a fortnight's time, when the old émigré at Tamporley and his servant plan to go with him.'

'We shall miss them,' said Miss Charity, looking tearful. 'The dear old Comte!'

'Oh, I daresay he will be back before long,' the Colonel consoled her. 'Now Boney is gone the Bourbons will be back on the throne of France, and for my part I don't envy that fat old king of theirs. He will be surrounded by reproachful faces, as the émigré's flock in, demanding the return of lands and properties that are no longer his to give, and the repayment of fortunes that were squandered on him and his brother There cannot be enough money in France to meet debts on so colossal a scale.'

'Poor M. Estoban!' sighed Miss Charity. 'I wonder if he ever will find his grand-son again?'

'He is an astute old gentleman,' commented the Colonel. 'When he plucked Philippe Cadot out of gaol he suggested that Squire Forsett should look among my officers for Miss Sophy's partner in her elopement, and at the end of a week of course they were found, Frank Woodcock and his bride of six days, in London. Strangely enough Beaumont was with them when the Squire arrived, threatening to horsewhip the young man, and it was Beaumont who poured oil on troubled waters and wined and dined the Squire and talked him into thinking at last that Sophy hadn't done such a bad thing after all.'

'But did you not know that Frank Woodcock had gone?' asked Melissa.

'Of course. The young devil asked for leave, "to attend a wedding" if you please, without a word of it being his own!'

Doverton was a dull place without Edward Beaumont, and the young officers from the militia which were all that Miss Charity and Mrs. Delaney could offer Melissa by way of consolation, were too young and stupid to entertain her. Their conversation centred round horses and dogs and their prospects now that the war had ended, and whether the militia would be disbanded at once. It was almost a relief when her Aunt Rebecca wrote to tell her that her father had been far from well, thus giving her an excuse to go home.

During the weeks before they left the Comte and his guest toured the neighbourhood together in the little pony chaise, bidding their friends goodbye. They left Tamporley to the last, and that afternoon Philippe Cadot did not accompany his host, making the excuse that he had friends to visit in the town.

M. Estoban came home to find his young friend sitting quietly in the salon, reading one of his books on philosophy.

'You find that interesting?' he said.

'But yes, Monsieur. Very interesting indeed.' But the Comte noticed that he had not got any further in his reading than the first few pages.

'I hope you found your friends well?' he said.

'I did not go.' The Lieutenant tried to laugh 'I detest leave-taking, Monsieur. Each goodbye sits on my heart like indigestion!'

The émigré understood him better than he thought. 'They were sorry not to see you at Tamporley,' he said. 'I was charged with messages for you . . . The Dowager wishes you a safe journey and Miss Cheriton wishes you all happiness in the future.'

Philippe said nothing. He seemed to be waiting for another message, and presently it came.

'Young Lady Tamporley came to see the Dowager just before I left . . . She asked me when we were leaving in the morning, and when I told her that we were catching the stage at noon for Salisbury, she said she would go down to the Tamporley woods early in the morning to see if there were any violets we could take with us. "You would like some English violets?" she said. "My dear," I told her, "they are the flowers of the late Emperor . . . but if you give them to me, how can I refuse to treasure them?" I said I would send you to the woods to fetch them before we left.'

'I may not be there,' said Philippe with a harsh little laugh. 'But no doubt Jeanne will be happy to be your messenger.'

M. Estoban put his hand for a moment on his shoulder. 'She will not make a scene,' he said gently. 'She only wants to say goodbye ... Perhaps the children will be with her.'

But she was alone when Philippe entered the Tamporley woods on the following morning. The April sky was overcast and the air was full of rain. He glanced at her thin shoes and said abruptly: 'Your feet are wet ... you should not have come.'

'But I had to see you.' She was like a child pleading for a last treat. 'Just once ... before you go.'

They sat down on the fallen log where they had sat in the past, and she held out the posy of violets that she had picked for him, and he took it and the hand that held it, and raised it, not to his lips, but to his cheek and kept it there, so that she felt the warm roughness of his face against her cold fingers. She knew that her life was ended, but she knew too that she had to meet what remained of it with courage, because it was no longer in her to be afraid. One had one's obligations, one's duty to do, and the way was clear now and as grey as the uncertain sky.

'Oh Philippe!' she said, her voice rough, her lips dry, as she tried to accept and not to rebel against it. 'Why did we meet so late? ... It was only a few years that separated us ... Why could we not meet before?'

'I knew when I saw you with the daffodils that I loved you,' he said. 'I shall love you till I die ...'

'My dear, you will marry ...'

'Marriage is a convenience ... I am talking about love.' He slipped to his knees beside her, his arms around her, his face in her lap, and her hand rested gently on his head, learning the wiry feel of the close curls, because this one moment must last her to eternity.

'My dearest love!' she whispered. This high romance, that glowed and glittered and was edged with gold, and hurt so deeply ... 'The chaise will be here ... You must go.'

He pulled her face down to his and kissed her roughly, not once but many times, and then he released her abruptly and scrambled up. As she saw him striding away from her and watched until he was lost in the trees she knew that she would see his shabby blue coat and the angle of the hat on his dark head for the rest of her life.

Jeanne and the luggage had gone on a farm cart to wait for the stage at the coach office in Doverton, and the chaise was ready, with the Comte at the reins and young Ted leading the fat pony for the last time. As Philippe climbed up, the old man glanced at his white face and said gently: 'You have said your goodbye?'

'Yes, thank you, Monsieur.' Philippe's voice was grim, his eyes darkly frowning.

'And nothing else?'

'Why should there be anything else, Monsieur?' Philippe looked at the little bunch of blue and white violets in his hand, seeing for the first time that they were bound with a golden hair. He thrust it away in his breast pocket, and started ahead of him, and the familiar road to Doverton became suddenly blurred. 'One does not seduce an angel,' he said, more to himself than to M. Estoban.

# 14

Melissa returned to the Rectory, assured of a rapturous welcome from Pom and a more restrained but equally affectionate one from her father and her aunt.

Doverton settled down into a placid existence, rarely touched by the outside world, but Miss Cheriton thought that her niece's letters lacked their usual gaiety and put it down to the Lieutenant's neglect to say goodbye to her before he left with the Comte.

'I thought Mr. Cadot would distract dear Mel's thoughts from her unlucky love affair at home,' she told the Dowager mournfully, 'but I am afraid now that perhaps I may have encouraged the acquaintance more than I should. And of course the dear Lieutenant was so very good-looking.'

'Yes, he was a handsome man,' agreed her sister, rather as if it were an extraordinary circumstance, good-looks being the natural prerogative of Englishmen. 'But I daresay Mel is only feeling dull at being at home again after our parties and gaiety here,' she went on consolingly. 'And then there was Sophy's elopement, which was so upsetting for everybody.'

'I don't see why it should be upsetting,' said Miss Cheriton querulously. 'I thought it was very romantic.'

'But then you see romance in everything,' said the Dowager. 'One excellent result of the business is that Mrs. Forsett will not now return to Tamporley. She has been waiting to manage her brother-in-law's household for him for years, and with

159

Sophy out of the way she will meet little opposition. He will be like butter in her hands.'

'Poor dear man,' said Miss Cheriton.

M. Estoban had arrived in London in time for Louis XVIII's triumphal entry into the town, and he wrote an enthusiastic account of the happy circumstance to the Dowager. The streets he said had been alive with white cockades and white tokens of the Bourbons, and everyone who had a white apron or a white shirt waved it at the windows as the King of France went by.

*I believe in his heart Philippe Cadot was very disappointed in our old King,* the Comte continued. *Republican as he is he will never admit to having any interest in His Majesty, but after he had gone by he remarked how fat and old he was and I had to remind him that His Majesty was the brother of King Louis XVI, and that he had been in exile for twenty-five years.*

He went on to describe the reception at Grillon's Hotel in Albemarle Street, at which the King had entertained all the émigrés that were left in England. They were disappointed that the Duchesse d'Angoulême was not there, but she spent the evening in South Audley Street with her father-in-law. The ladies' dresses were charming, M. Estoban told his old friend, but there were of course no jewels to be seen, and some of the gentlemen were so shabby as to be ludicrous. But the King was graciousness itself, although he must have been tired after the excitement of the day. He wished he could have taken Philippe there: it might have changed his views on French aristocracy.

They sailed in two days' time for France, in company with many others. Philippe might have gone ahead if he had chosen, but he had the absurd notion that the Comte and his old servant might need looking after on the journey.

Miss Cheriton related all this news to Melissa when she wrote to her, adding that Mrs. Forsett had spent a few days at Tamporley while the Squire was in town and that her visit had caused Tam to fly in to such rages that Sarah had taken to her bed again and even Miss Pope was in a Nervous State.

The Rector was considerably better when this letter arrived and Melissa had been reading it to him when she noticed that he had fallen asleep. She put the letter away and had taken up her needlework when she happened to glance up and through the window she saw a gentleman on horseback in the act of dismounting at the Rectory gate. A groom was with him and he handed the horse's bridle to the man and opened the gate and began to walk up towards the house as if he were not quite sure of his welcome there.

'Oh!' said Melissa in a voice that was full of delight. The handkerchief that was spread over her father's face still rose and fell with the Rector's steady breathing and she dropped her needlework and seized Pom in case he greeted the visitor unkindly, and ran to the door to open it before he could knock.

'My dear Miss Melissa!' said Edward Beaumont. 'Is anything wrong?'

'No . . . that is my father has been ill and as he was asleep I was afraid that Pom might wake him.' She stroked Pom soothingly because he was regarding the visitor with his old suspicion.

'Why, then, the Rectory garden is large, and it is a fine day,' said Mr. Beaumont smiling. 'Could we not take a turn on the lawn?'

She said she would enjoy it and she ran to fetch her hat and joined him a few minutes later, and they walked across the lawn together with Pom sniffing at their heels, and found their way to a seat beneath a spreading cedar tree.

'I was so sorry,' she said then, as they sat down. 'About Sophy marrying someone else as she did . . . and in that way . . . '

'Oh, but I helped her to do it. Did she not tell you?' He

laughed at the expression on her face. 'When I met Miss Sophy in London she confided in me that she was in love with a young Captain in the militia in Doverton, and that her father and aunt had refused to let her meet any young man without money, being convinced that they were all fortune hunters and between us we devised a scheme to outwit them. I would visit my old friends the Halsteads at Dove Tye and she would sing my praises so that anyone would imagine that my interest was in her, and directly she reached the age of twenty-one she and her adoring young Captain could elope together. I would add that we were helped considerably in our schemes by Philippe Cadot, to whom Frank paid innumerable morning calls while he was a guest in the old Comte's house at Tamporley, and where Miss Sophy was able to meet him under the pretext of having extra French conversation lessons from M. Estoban. The night after the ball Frank took her straight to my sister's house in London and she was married from there to her gallant Captain a few days later. In the meantime however I had been making discreet enquiries about her father's business matters, being almost sure that it was not the loss of his daughter that had frightened him, but the loss of her fortune. I soon discovered that he had been borrowing on the expectation of her money coming into his possession when she was twenty-one, and when he arrived in London, breathing vengeance on the young people I visited him at his hotel, told him what I knew, and suggested that he settled his mortgaged house on his daughter, or sold it to pay his debt to her and retired with his sister-in-law to Bath. He was quite reasonable once he had got over the shock of my information and it is now his intention to leave Doverton for Bath . . . Sophy is purchasing a small estate near my own in Norfolk, and I am looking forward to having them as my neighbours.'

'Dear Sophy!' said Melissa softly.

'She is a very nice girl,' agreed Mr. Beaumont, staring at the lawn and prodding a daisy root with his riding crop. 'And if I had not happened to have an unfortunately constant nature

I might have been tempted to oust Frank in the lady's affections . . . But the fact is, Mel, that when I asked somebody to marry me last Christmas and she refused me . . .'

'Which she regretted the moment after she had done it,' said Melissa mournfully.

'And when I saw her in Doverton recently and she was so much kinder than she had been . . .'

'Because she was so sorry and ashamed for what she did . . .'

'I was encouraged to come and put the same question to her again, in case she might have changed her mind.' He turned his head and saw the answer in her eyes, and possessed himself of her hands while Pom fell upon the unsuspecting daisy root and dug it up furiously.

The Rector, waking from his sleep, looked out of the window and saw the groom and the two horses at the gate, and, being puzzled as to whom his caller could be, went to a side window and saw his daughter being embraced by a young man under the cedar tree, while Pom dug a large hole in the lawn.

'God bless my soul,' said the Rector, astonished. 'Edward Beaumont back again!' And then, 'So that was what has been making Mel so unhappy since she has been home . . . And there was I and Rebecca thinking it must be Charity's Romantic Frenchman!'

\*　　\*　　\*

Having reached Paris Philippe Cadot left M. Estoban and his old servant in lodgings in the Rue de Suresnes, and went on to his uncle's house on the outskirts of the city and attempted to fit himself into the niche from which his service in the Emperor's army had plucked him. But the regiment in which he had served was disbanded, he had lost touch with the studies that had been interrupted, and in fact he was no longer sure that the life of an attorney was as attractive as it had seemed in the past. He fell into a restless habit of going into the town every day and dropping into the Comte's lodgings, and he was annoyed because his uncle and aunt sent no message of thanks for all the old man had done for him. He felt that their neglect was unkind, to say the least of it, although he was forced to admit that their incivility did not appear to be noticed by his old friend.

The truth was that M. Estoban had other things on his mind, and as he joined the other émigrés in the royal salon at the Tuileries he found himself jostled out of the way by a number of new barons, all using the coveted 'de' to which they had no manner of right, and whose honours and positions and wealth had been gained under the Emperor.

It seemed to the Comte that not only was the King anxious to retain the good-will of such people, but they were equally anxious to purchase his interest with far more money than the noblemen who had followed him into exile had set eyes on in the last twenty-five years, while as for the fortune that M. Estoban himself had poured out in the Bourbon cause, it had simply become a bad debt that would neither be recovered nor mentioned.

There were compensations to be found however in the King's kindly notice of him, and if he had possessed a son he might have been able to interest His Majesty in promoting him to a post in the new government. But alone and old and poor as he was, the most he could hope for as recompense were the Croix de Guerre and the Legion of Honour, and on these Jeanne poured scorn and wrath when Philippe called on the day after they had bestowed on her master.

'That will make a good dinner!' she said, her hands on her hips and her black eyes flashing. 'That will pay the rent of our lodgings indeed!'

'But surely the King knows that M. le Comte ruined himself for him and his family?' protested Philippe, equally dismayed. 'He was in Condé's army . . .'

'Monsieur, it is said in Paris that for every thousand gentlemen of France who left to join the Prince's army, five thousand have returned!' Jeanne's voice shook with anger. 'If you were to question these so-called barons who are crowding round His Majesty now you would find that *all* of them would have served in the Prince's army . . . when it is well understood that they hid their heads under mountains of documents for fear of having them taken off! They would not lift a finger to help anybody but themselves!'

Philippe found that his friendship for M. Estoban met with disapproval at home.

'You have been to see your émigré again?' his aunt said one day scornfully. 'I should have thought you had seen enough of that old man by this time!'

'He was kind to me in England,' Philippe pointed out. 'I like to show some sort of gratitude for what he did.'

His aunt tossed her head, reading a reproach into the words. 'You accompanied him back to Paris, found a lodging for him and eased the journey for him and his old servant,' she said, her voice rising shrilly. 'That was a sufficient return for what he had done for you. Nothing more is necessary!'

'Your aunt is right, Philippe,' said the lawyer gravely. 'These Royalists will have nothing to do with us now they are home again. It is said in the city that they have learnt nothing and have forgotten nothing in the years that they have been away, and for my part I believe it to be true.' He saw the expression on the young man's face and continued: 'Yesterday I had promised to meet a client in the Luxembourg gardens, and as I waited for him there I observed a group of these old people. The ladies were seated in a circle gossiping, and the gentlemen leaned on the back of their chairs, listening, and do you know what the conversation was about? Not about the difficulties the King must face in forming his government now he is back among us, not about the foreign armies that over-run our country now that Bonaparte is defeated and in Elba, not even about the great Duke of Wellington, who rules us all with much more vigour than any king could do. No, their conversation was entirely confined to the Royal family, and how charming they were, and what a good appetite the King had for his food, and how charming was Madame Angoulême, and how enchanting it was to watch a family that was so devoted ...'

'I am glad to find that they consider the Duchesse d'Angoulême so charming, with her sour face!' cried Madame Cadot.

'To me it is a sad face,' said Philippe. 'Not sour ... And who can blame her for it? Her memories of Paris and its people cannot be happy ones ...'

'You have been talking to your old émigré again!' His aunt tried to laugh at him for being so partisan.

'On the contrary M. le Comte never mentions the King or the Duchesse or the Princess. I think, like many others, he is disappointed with the attitude of the King towards his old friends, but he is too loyal to say so.'

'When you see M. Estoban tomorrow then you may remind him that it is only the Imperialists round the King who give him his popularity in the eyes of the people, and émigrés like himself are regarded as necessary evils because they followed the King and he could not shake them off. But by the citizens of Paris these old Royalists are neither liked nor pitied.'

'M. le Comte does not ask for pity or for liking,' said Philippe. 'And I shall not be seeing him tomorrow as he is going into the country to visit the Estoban estates.

His uncle changed colour. 'But there is nothing of them left!' he cried. 'They have all been disposed of to others years ago!'

Philippe studied him thoughtfully, wondering why he was so put out. 'Have you had anything to do with the Estoban estates then?' he asked.

'No ... of course not. But it is the usual thing.' And M. Cadot began to talk of other things.

When the Comte started on his journey on the following

day he knew as well as M. Cadot did that the Estoban estates had been seized as National property after the Revolution, but although his journey held a quest that he knew to be hopeless, he felt he must make one final return to the past before he turned his back on it for ever.

He found the village at the gates of the château changed in a strangely subtle way. The windowless cottages had gone and the new ones were lighted by neat sashes instead of depending on an open door. The houses were built of brick, although here and there he recognised stones from the old château incorporated in the brickwork, the thatches were well kept, and the small plots of land that surrounded the houses were carefully tended by their owners and their families.

He looked for familiar faces in the villagers and could find none. The rags and the bare feet of the old days too were missing: the villagers themselves were well-dressed and well-fed, and there was not one of them without a pair of shoes.

He put up at the *auberge*, a clean house with clean beds and good food, and there was nobody there who knew or cared about the Estobans. He called himself M. Brisson and said he was a traveller on his way through France, and on the second day of his stay he made his way to the château.

The avenue leading from the village to the old house was an over-grown track, the limes that had formed a scented archway in the summer-time had been cut down, and of the château itself only the gateway and the fifteenth-century chapel remained.

It was difficult to secure one moment from the past in such a wilderness where even the chapel was open to the sky, and he returned sadly to the village and found the *aubergiste* busy folding up sheets of excellent quality and colour. He congratulated her on her house linen and the woman, a comely creature in her early fifties, smiled and said that the sheets belonged to her daughter, who was to marry a farmer in a few weeks' time.

167

'She has now over fifty pairs of sheets,' she added proudly. 'And they will not go far enough to provide beds for the labourers in harvest time.'

M. Estoban listened in polite astonishment. In his day the farmers as well as their labourers slept on straw.

His hostess studied him thoughtfully over the sheets. He was obviously one of the *ancien régime* – you could tell that by his powdered hair and antiquated clothes – but the sadness in his face touched her. She said, 'You have been visiting the old château perhaps, M'sieu?'

'Yes.' He asked if anything was known about the family who had lived there.

'It is said, I believe, that M. le Comte and his sons perished fighting with Condé's army, and that his family . . . ' A shrug and an eloquent spread of hands continued the story. 'Parbleu, it was in Paris during The Terror, you understand. I had been told that the ladies all died there.'

'But the little boy . . . was nothing heard about him?' Painfully he waited for her reply.

'That I know nothing about.' She shook her head decidedly. 'You see, M'sieu, when the château was destroyed the village was burned too, and those in it were murdered, unless they had the good fortune to escape while there was time. There is nobody here now who remembers anything about the Estoban family.' He looked so downcast that she took him for a friend of the old family that had lived at the château, and she cast about in her mind as to whom she knew who could help him, finally remembering a Madame Heriot who had been a servant at the château in the old days and now lived with her married son on his farm outside the village.

She pointed out the direction he should take and he thanked her and started out briskly and in a very short while came upon a cottage belonging to a small-holder, enclosed in a low mud wall in which there was a smaller cottage belonging to the old lady. In the yard a cow, a mule and a pig were sharing

168

the shelter of a shed, on the roof of which flax was drying in the sun.

Madame Heriot was seated in the doorway of her house making a shirt for her grand-child, and returned his polite greeting smilingly, shading her eyes from the sun to study him more closely.

He was making enquiries, he said, about the family who had lived at the château, but he got no further. She got up with a smothered cry of pleasure, put the shirt on one side, and took his hand in both of hers.

'M'sieu, you are not . . . you cannot be M. le Comte?' she said, her voice shaking and tears starting to her eyes.

He found himself absurdly overcome by her emotion, and for a man who never showed his feelings tears for him too were very near the surface.

'But yes, Madame . . . but I am here for no other reason than to try and find news of my grand-son.'

'Ah yes, he was travelling in the second carriage, the berline that disappeared.' She asked him in and provided a chair for him and called her own small grand-son from the yard and told him to find an egg – a nice brown one – for M'sieu. M. Estoban noticed the clean and lofty bed given pride of place in the outer room, and the pieces of old china on some shelves and a few books. Certainly these peasants had travelled far from the days when he and his friends had ridden through that field of corn . . .

'You know what happened to the berline, Madame?' he asked.

'Ah M'sieu, there is nothing good that I can tell you about it. You see, in that carriage with the little boy and his *bonne* there travelled the jewels, and it was well-known that many of the coaches in which there were jewellery and valuables never reached Paris . . . But I know where that berline is now.'

'The same one, Madame?'

'But yes, M. le Comte, the second carriage . . . It is in

the farm-yard of a house at a village called St. Leon, where the forest comes down to meet the road.'

'St. Leon? But that is not on the road to Paris . . . '

'No. It is to the right of the St. Leon cross-roads, and it is that road that the carriage took. When it was found it was in the forest, pulled up into a bridle path, and it was empty. It had rotted there for many years I believe before the farmer took the wheels for his cart and the body of the carriage to make into a hen-house, and that is where it is now.'

'I understand.' The Comte had never expected anything else to come of his enquiries, and yet now that it was certain and that expectation had been confirmed, his heart felt cold and dead. He said stiffly, 'The coachman took the wrong turning in the darkness, and they were set upon and robbed and murdered . . . '

'I am afraid that is the case.' She wiped her eyes and tried to console him with what bleak comfort she had to offer. 'There were many carriages left abandoned on the road in those days, M'sieu, and many bodies left in the ditches . . . One did not ask how they died.'

He thought of a frightened little boy, facing Heaven only knew what fate . . . and a young girl of seventeen, hands tied behind her, mounting a tumbril . . . It was not good, that, surely, to terrify children before one killed them? He thanked the old lady and got up heavily to go on his way, and then suddenly she thought of something else.

'Somebody came down here enquiring also after your family soon after The Terror was ended, M. le Comte. It was many years ago now . . . He said he was a lawyer from Paris, and he was asking questions about the family and about your grandson in particular . . . I did not trust him and so I told him nothing. But he wrote down his name on a piece of paper and I have it still. Perhaps M'sieu would like to have it.'

'Thank you, Madame.' He waited and she went to a dresser where there was a small wooden box and took out of it a faded piece of paper and gave it to him. He thanked her again and went on his way, without waiting for the brown eggs that were being searched for by her little grand-son, but it was not until he was on his way back to Paris that he troubled himself to look at it.

And the name on the paper was that of M. Raoul Cadot, at the address that Philippe had given him on his own in Paris.

# 15

On the journey M. Estoban found his thoughts returning
once or twice to Philippe's uncle with a feeling of grim amusement. Contrary to the young man's ideas he had not failed to
notice the senior Cadot's lack of courtesy, and now he suddenly
thought he knew why he had been so anxious to avoid him.
It was no doubt because he had been one of the lawyers employed by the government to sequester the Estoban estates
and dispose of them to the small-holders and farmers who
had them now. Well, surely he should have known that he
would not be blamed for that? A man had his work to do,
he supposed, and it was not possible that M. Cadot had had
much choice.

When he reached his lodgings in Paris on the following
evening he found old Jeanne waiting for him in a state of
great excitement. There had been a gentleman to see him,
and a command for him to call upon His Majesty directly
he returned from the country.

'An audience, eh?' said the Comte. 'We are progressing,
it seems.'

'No doubt it is to be a reward at last for all you have done,'
the old servant said. 'I have made ready the Court dress, M'sieu,
and I have polished the sword – it is all ready and waiting
to be put on . . . While you dress, I will send the porter for a
carriage.'

'Very well.' He was tired to the bone and would have wel-
comed nothing so warmly as his bed but a royal command

could not be delayed, and he consented to change and to take himself in the hired carriage to the Tuileries.

There he presented himself to the King, who received him with his usual kindness, and after questioning him about his journey and expressing his sorrow when the Comte admitted that his fears for his grand-son had proved to be only too well-founded, he startled him by offering him a post at Naples.

M. Estoban did not hesitate to accept it. He would have felt more at home if it had been England to which he was to be sent, but everyone knew the weather in England was terrible and the damp, cold climate bad for old bones. He yearned for sunshine, and this he would surely find in Italy, and he had no regrets in parting from his old friends in Paris.

For the Comte there had been the other side of the picture in the Luxembourg Gardens. He knew that the Royalists who congregated there in the afternoons in their tight little circles, letting nobody in, shutting out everybody except their own kind, when night came retired to their poor lodgings and played cards sometimes by the light of one candle, still dressed in their threadbare uniforms and their old-fashioned dresses and suits of clothes, because there was no money to buy any more. The Comte had no wish to join these old people, without hope and without a future, and the day before he left Paris he took a carriage out to the district where the Cadots lived.

He recognised the lawyer's house at once from Philippe's description of it: it was a modest house of nice proportions, with green shutters at the windows, and at the side of the house the branches of an old vine with bunches of grapes that a gentleman in a gardener's apron was busy thinning out with a pair of scissors.

M. Estoban left the carriage and entered by the side door and the man in the gardener's apron saw him and the scissors fell to the ground.

'Monsieur?' he said, and the Comte was interested to see that he had gone very white. He felt impatience with the man for his fear of him: what after all was there to be afraid of

173

in the sale of an émigré's lands? Even if there was some legal hole that could be found in the contract he was not the one to look for it after all these years.

'My name is Estoban,' he said coldly. 'I have come to see Philippe and to say goodbye to him, because I leave Paris for Naples tomorrow.'

M. Cadot stared at him without speaking: he appeared to be thinking deeply, and then he removed his apron, picking up the scissors and asked him to do him the honour of entering the house. He conducted him to a pleasant salon, simply furnished, and filled with a cool, green light from the hanging vine outside.

He begged his guest to be seated and sent a servant to fetch his wife and in a few moments Madame came, a bustling little woman with dark, suspicious eyes.

Her husband introduced her. 'This is M. le Comte d'Estoban, my dear. He was so good to Philippe.'

'Ah yes. Bonjour, Monsieur.' She gave him a short ungracious bow, which he scarcely troubled himself to return. It was difficult to think that this couple, so bourgeois, so ordinary, could be related to Philippe, but there it was.

M. Cadot said in a troubled voice, 'I do not know what you can have thought of us – of my wife and myself, Monsieur – for not having come to thank you for the care you took of our nephew in England.'

'Thank you, Monsieur,' said the Comte coldly. 'I did not think about it at all. I have come to say goodbye to your nephew today, not to beg for thanks. None are needed or expected.'

Madame flushed fierily and said that she would send the servant to them with some wine and bustled away and a look that she gave her husband at the door sent him hurrying after her.

'He is just what I told you he would be,' she said in an angry whisper. 'Cold and proud . . . You will not tell him, will you?'

174

'My dear, I must . . . My conscience will not let me do otherwise.'

'Your conscience! My God, what use is that to Philippe? He has not to live with it.'

'No, but I have, and it troubles me too much for me to ignore it.'

'Then you are a bigger fool than I took you for . . This man will never thank you, and neither will poor Philippe.'

'Yet I must do what is right.' He went back into the salon and in a few minutes the servant came with the wine but Madame stayed away.

The wine was soft and pleasing to the Comte's palate and he reflected that M. Cadot might have made a better wine-merchant than a lawyer. He waited politely for him to speak and was surprised when he turned his back on him and walked to the window.

'The fact is, Monsieur,' he said, speaking hoarsely and rather fast, 'my wife and I have not known what to do. We have talked about this affair ever since we knew who it was who had helped to mend Philippe's broken head. It was the strangest chance that sent him to you that day, as strange as the chance that sent him to me more than twenty years ago.'

The wine had soothed the Comte's ruffled spirits, but he objected to conducting a conversation with a man's back.

'Sit down opposite me here,' he directed. 'And tell me what it is that you want to say to me.'

The lawyer poured himself out some wine with a hand that shook: it was evident that he was very much distressed and M. Estoban was more puzzled still.

'It was during The Terror,' M. Cadot said. 'My brother and I had always been anxious for a reform of the constitution: we had hoped great things from the States General when it was formed, but we wanted nothing more than a democratic assembly under the King. I want you to believe this, Monsieur.'

The Comte said nothing. His face was quite expressionless: it was evident that the opinions of M. Cadot and his brother were of not the slightest concern to him, and the little man's heart failed him. Was his wife right after all? Was it indeed possible to expect sympathy of any kind from this old émigré? But having embarked on his story there was no turning back.

'I suppose the truth was that we were both republicans at heart however, and although when the Revolution broke I left Paris and took my wife into the country until things should become quieter, my brother continued with activities that took him down steeper and more dangerous paths. I lost touch with him, indeed it was no longer safe to correspond with him, but I was horrified to learn when The Terror was at its height that he and his young wife had been arrested and taken to prison.'

He paused but again his visitor made no comment. His silence indicated that he had heard these things before and from a far more terrible angle than that experienced by M. Cadot and his brother. The lawyer continued, making an effort at self-control, 'I went back to Paris for three days to see if I could find there any old friends among the madmen who directed the Revolution at that time, to prevail upon them, if I could, to obtain my brother's release.'

His thoughts went back to those terrifying days and nights, still like a half-remembered nightmare, when Paris had been a dead city and given over to death, when anybody with a clean face was suspect, and when citizens went to bed directly it was dark because there were no candles left in the city, and a lighted room could bring a patrol on them at any moment, demanding who it was they might be entertaining at that hour. He would have liked to have told the Comte something of all this, about the dangers of being in the streets after dark, and how people trembled in their beds, waiting for the knock on the street door that would mean arrest and death, but he felt such confidences would not be appreciated. There was no feeling at all in that cold face. He went on, as lightly as he could, 'I remember how difficult it was to obtain lodgings, because you had to show your passport before you would be given a room anywhere, and before you could leave the city you had to have that passport visa-ed by the Revolutionary Committee of the section you happened to be in.'

There were forty-eight of those committees, each cne more eager than the last to clap you into prison and feed you to the guillotine: he wondered if perhaps M. Estoban would appreciate that? He did not think so. He continued more lightly still: 'You will see, I think, that a visit to Paris presented unusual hazards just then.'

The Comte sipped his wine. Nothing of this had anything to do with him and he was wondering why M. Cadot appeared to be so anxious to talk about an era of which no self-respecting Frenchman could be exactly proud.

'I soon discovered that my old friends had either fled or proved their equality with others on the guillotine.' M. Cadot seemed to be determined that he should know it all. 'My brother's house was under guard, the doors bearing the seals of the Committee of Public Safety, and when I made my way to the prison where he and his wife were lodged I found that they were already under sentence of death, and my request to see them for the last time was brusquely refused. It was as I was turning away from the prison that a woman with a little boy spoke to me. She asked me where she could discover the names of the people who had died. I said it would be impossible – there were too many of them. She then told me that she was looking for the family of the little boy, that she had been to their house in the Faubourg St. Germain and that it had been taken over by one of the city's committees and she dare not ask the rough men there what had happened to its owners. "I don't know what to do with the child," she said. "It was this promise I made to his *bonne*, do you see, when she was dying. She begged me to take him to Paris, to his family, and I said that I would the next time my husband had a load of vegetables for the market." She was a farmer's wife, and very poor and it was seldom that they had a load to spare but they had arrived the day before and had put up with her husband's brother, who had a greengrocer's shop. She was to return there that afternoon, when it was hoped that the farmer would have disposed of his vegetables at a good profit and she would have disposed of the child.

'She then told me a garbled story of how the child was the grand-son of a nobleman who had emigrated, leaving his family at his château in the country, from which they had been forced to fly when a rabble started marching on them. The ladies set out for Paris in three carriages, and the middle one, in which were travelling the little boy and his *bonne*, left the others at the end of the second day's journey and made its way about three kilometres or so into hilly, wooded lonely country. The *bonne* had told the farmer's wife that she had thought at first that the coachman had lost his way, as it was getting dark and the roads they had been travelling until then had been crowded, but after a time he stopped the coach and got down and ordered her out with the boy and told her to run up into the woods with him if she didn't want to have their throats cut. The terrified girl took the little boy with her and hid in the trees to see what the man was doing: she said that the coachman and the groom un-harnessed the horses, and the two women who were travelling in the coach in charge of the family's jewels joined them, and the four of them rode off together, taking the valuables with them.

'The *bonne* was a country girl and she had no money. She dare not try to find the crowded main road to Paris in the dark, and so she wrapped the child in a shawl and they passed the night in the coach. In the morning she started off on foot with a very tired and hungry little boy.'

Here M. Cadot paused and stole a glance at M. Estoban, and he saw that he had put down his wine half-finished and was shading his eyes with his hand. He hurried on:

'The farmer's wife told me that she did not know how long they had been on the road by the time they reached her husband's farm, but she thought it must have taken them months to make the journey. The poor girl told her that she had just followed the stream of people, begging a lift for the child when she could, and food from the few farms that were still occupied as they passed. Sometimes she stopped and worked a week or two for their keep, sometimes they were reduced to eating turnips from the fields, and on several occasions the child suffered acutely from dysentery. When they reached the farm they were allowed to sleep in the barn where there was some hay, but in the morning the child came to them and said that his *bonne* was asleep and that he could not wake her up. The farmer's wife hurried to the barn and found her lying there with small-pox on her and quite unconscious, and although she had children of her own who might catch the disease the good woman burnt the boy's clothes, bathed him and dressed him in some of her children's clothes and kept him with them until the girl died a few weeks later. By that time the child was running happily barefoot in the fields, helping the boys to tend the goats and the girls to feed the geese, and he looked upon them as his new family until, as I said, there was this load of vegetables ready for the market . . . Well, what was I to do? What would you have done, Monsieur? The woman was burdened with children of her own, and one more mouth to feed meant a great deal to her and her husband. I had nobody left now that my brother and his wife were to die, and so I decided that I would take the child to my wife in the country and we would see what could be done to find his family later.

'I brought him out of Paris on the diligence the next day and he remained with us. We had no children of our own, and we called him our nephew, giving him my dead brother's name, Philippe. He knows nothing of his history, except that his parents perished during The Terror, and that he is my nephew and my adopted son.'

The lawyer noticed that although the Comte sat as if he were listening to a voice from a past in which he had no part he was still shading his eyes with his hand, and he took heart from it. Perhaps the old man was not entirely without feelings after all.

'I don't want you to think that I did not try to find his relatives,' he went on gently. 'I did everything I could to discover if there were any left. But his mother's family had gone – the Marquis d'Arblon was arrested during the September massacres and cut to pieces outside the Abbaye prison. His father and uncle had died, and his grandfather had disappeared. It was thought that he had gone to England – in an open boat, some said. I travelled to England, though it was not easy, and I made enquiries from the old Bishop of St. Pol in London who knew most of the émigrés there, and he sent me to an old lady and her husband living in abject poverty in two rooms in St. George's Fields. The old lady was paralysed and could tell me nothing, the old gentleman had died of starvation the week before I arrived, and the servant – a Breton woman – spat in my face and told me that the old lady was the last of her family. "You have murdered the rest," she said. "Why do you come asking after them now? Will you never be satisfied or do you want to drag her back to France to feed her to your guillotine?" I shall never forget her face as she said it . . . I did not stop to tell her about the boy. I felt he would have a better chance with us than in such a household as that and besides, we had grown fond of him.' He stopped and took another gulp of wine.

'And the family's name?' said M. Estoban inimically.

'Your own, M. le Comte.'

'So Philippe is my grand-son?'

'Yes, Monsieur, I believe so with all my heart.'

'And you say that he knows nothing of all this?'

'Nothing . . . As I said, I have not known what to do.'

'I should have thought your duty was plain.'

The lawyer glanced quickly at the old man's implacable face. 'You mean . . . I should tell him?'

'What other course is open to you?'

'But Monsieur . . . ' The little man spread his hands, his

180

eyes full of tears. 'We have brought him up as our son . . .
He is a good Frenchman, neither republican nor royalist,
good-hearted and kind . . . He will make an excellent lawyer,
once he has conquered this restlessness that he has brought
home from the war, because he has a sound head on his
shoulders. His life will be prosperous, assured, contented . . .
What, in contrast, have you to offer him, M. le Comte? Tell
me that, if you please!'

The words were more anguished than defiant, and behind
them there was an agony of love for the child that he and
his wife had taken into their home more than twenty years
ago but the Comte's thoughts were not upon them, but only
upon his grand-son, Philippe.

He remembered the games of chess and the slender hands
that had moved among the chessmen, the face that was as
handsome as his own sons' faces, the brain that was clear
and sound and capable of appreciating far wider horizons
and broader visions than those of an attorney's practice. But
as Cadot himself said, what indeed could he give Philippe
in exchange for this bourgeois life that he offered his adopted
son? Ruined estates, an empty title, and an income that de-
pended on the whims of whatever monarch happened to be
on the throne of France, and perhaps as the years built up
behind him, a bitterness and a sour regret for the things he
had never known.

He recalled the children of the émigrés in England and
the high hopes their parents had for them when they had
returned, hopes of what had proved to be but empty honours
in this new France. When he died, Philippe would become
the Comte d'Estoban, but what was the use of that if only
bitterness went with it? It was in his mind that he would
rather see his grand-son a peasant than bourgeois, a class
that he and his kind hated more than any other. But sitting
there in the salon in the green light shed by the trailing vine
on the walls outside, M. Estoban turned things over slowly
in his mind and found that he was not sure of anything any

more. He was getting old and tired, and his brain was not so active now: it took longer for him to think things out. He would have liked to ask advice on such an important question, but there was nobody to ask. He was the only one who could decide.

If there were only some middle path that he and Philippe might tread together, a path leading between the utter dullness of the Cadots, good people as they were, and the elbowing, the pushing, the waiting like a lackey in the ante-chambers of the royal palace for favours that would be in the end bestowed on richer and more fortunate young men! M. Estoban and grief were old acquaintances now, one might almost say, old friends, but he did not wish his grand-son to be hampered by sorrowing for lost fortunes, for vanished estates, for past glories that he had never known. He must do better than that.

He said aloud, as if answering those inner thoughts, 'For me and my people it was always "Vive le Roi," as it is still, but for Philippe and his children in the future it may be "Vive la France," which is perhaps much better. Who can tell?' He got stiffly to his feet. 'You have kept his secret for twenty years, M. Cadot, and I daresay I can trust you to keep it for as many more?'

'You do not mean to claim him?' The relief in the little man's face was enormous.

'But for what purpose?' The Comte's shoulders lifted in a shrug. 'As you yourself said just now, Monsieur, what have I to offer him?'

M. Cadot bowed low. He could only find a mumble of acknowledgement for such magnanimity, while a final, wretched resentment seized him because this penniless old émigré was exhibiting a generosity that he knew to be utterly beyond his own powers, and by the cool, amused gleam in the old man's eyes he knew that he had guessed his feelings.

And then suddenly everything was altered, and in one

moment, Philippe's future was resolved. There came a step in the hall outside, the door was thrown open and he was there.

'M. le Comte!' He came to him gladly. 'I called at your lodgings and Jeanne told me the good news, but she did not know where you had gone. Had I dreamed you would be here I'd have hurried home.'

'It is of no consequence, but I am glad to see you before I leave for Italy tomorrow.'

'You go so soon?' His dismay warmed the old man's heart.

'The appointment has been offered and I must take it. Also I shall find the sunshine in Naples: I have been without it far too long during my years in England.'

'No more hired carriages,' exulted Philippe. 'You will have your own carriage . . . you will drive in state, with your out-riders and your servants! Oh, how I would like to be there to see it!' He smiled down at M. Estoban, half-wistful, half-serious. 'You will not find yourself in need of a secretary while you are there I suppose?'

'A secretary?' The Comte did not glance at the lawyer although he caught the whistling breath he drew, and suddenly he laughed. It was a laugh of amusement for his own stupidity in not having thought of it before, of triumph because it was the one, irrefutable argument to which the Cadots could find no answer, and of joy because he and Philippe would not have to be parted after having found each other for so short a time. 'My dear boy,' he said, 'give me one month to settle myself and to discover in which way you can serve me – and France – best, and then I will write to you and ask you to come.'

'You mean that?' The delight in the boy's face wiped out the twenty lost years as if they had never been. 'You are really serious, Monsieur?'

'I have never been more serious, Philippe. I will teach you diplomacy, and the manners of the *ancien régime*, and in return you shall teach me an understanding of the new France and its people. Between us we will set your feet firmly on the ladder and who knows? The day may come when the name of – Cadot – is as well known in France as that of Bonaparte!'

'I will wait for your letter!' cried Philippe.

'It will not be long in coming.' M. Estoban bowed to the lawyer. 'Your servant, Monsieur! My regards to Madame!' And then, with a sudden quick movement, he took a grip on Philippe's hands, kissed him on both cheeks, and went out to the waiting carriage and was gone.

That night in their bedroom Madame said to her husband, 'So we have lost Philippe, and this aristocrat has won. I should have known it. You were no match for him. They always get their way in the end.' Her husband did not reply and she went on, 'He will tell him of course.'

'No,' said the lawyer decidedly. 'He will not tell him, and neither will we. Of that I am very sure.' After a moment he added, 'If I know M. Estoban he will be punctilious in paying his debts. When he comes to Paris Philippe will come with him, and he will be sent to pay his respects to his bourgeois relations, and I daresay from time to time M. Estoban will accompany him to tell us how well our nephew is progressing. I hope he will not come, mind you, because I hate him even more than he can hate me. But between us is this bridge – Philippe – and neither of us will destroy it, as long as we live.'

M. Estoban, back in his lodgings and watching while Jeanne packed, drew his ring from his finger and examined it smilingly. It was no longer only a symbol of the past: the future was there too in its glittering depths.

'I shall leave it to Philippe when I die,' he said.

'What!' Jeanne looked up sharply. 'You are speaking of that ring, M. le Comte?'

'Of course.'

'But . . . ' She was scandalised. 'That ring, Monsieur . . . '

'Has always belonged to the Estobans, ma bonne,' he finished for her. 'I know . . . it is handed down from one to the other. It is well . . . Proceed with your work.' And as she proceeded, he composed himself to sleep.

\* \* \*

One warm day at the beginning of September Lady Tamporley received a letter from M. Estoban. In it he thanked her for her friendship and for the friendship of her family, and he told her that he had left the toy drummers that the children loved so much in the cabinet in his salon at the cottage. He would not be coming to England again, and he had instructed his man of affairs in Doverton to sell what little furniture remained there, except for his books, which were to be sent to him in Naples, and the toy drummers, which he would be obliged if she would accept for the children.

He added that on the day before he left for Naples he had seen Philippe Cadot, and had arranged for him to follow him later in the month.

*It is a life for which he is perfectly suited*, he concluded. *And I hope that we shall each set out to conquer our new worlds with sympathy and understanding. I am happy to have such a charming young man as M. Cadot with me. It is as if I had found the grand-son for whom I have been searching so long. My adieus and my blessings go with you, Madame, and with your enchanting family.*

Sarah went down through the park that afternoon to the cottage where the old émigré had lived with his servant, and where for a time Miss Cheriton's Romantic Frenchman had joined them. She let herself in with the key that was hanging inside the game-larder by the back-door, and she walked through the empty rooms sadly, remembering the many hours they had all spent there with the dear old man.

185

She found the toy drummers in the cabinet and carried them off with her, but before she left she went up the stairs to the room where she had seen Philippe, and it was emptier than any other room in the little house.

'Surely,' he said that day, 'you came on a sunbeam . . . '

She walked back through the woods and sat for a time on the fallen tree trunk, and the violets were lost now in the long grass, and other flowers were blooming there instead. White stitchwort, blue birds' eye, pink ragged robin and scarlet poppies and yellow bedstraw: all the flowers of late summer had taken over from the shy violets of March and April, and had made short work of their brief flowering and swept them away like an invading army. The feeling of desolation that had been with her since Philippe left came back again, so that her heart ached and the tears came.

She wiped them away and walked back slowly to the house, making her way to the little morning-room beyond the great library, and heard Tam come into the house and ask the servants where she was. He followed her into the morning-rom, impatient because she had not been there when he wanted her.

'Sarah!' he shouted from force of habit, and then he remembered that she did not like him to shout at her, and he went up to her and said her name more quietly, and she turned her head and he saw that her eyes were wet. 'What is the matter?' he asked, astonished. 'Dammit, Sarah, you've been crying!'

'I went down to the Comte's little house to fetch this toy for the children, and the house seemed so desolate and empty . . . ' Tears welled up again in the flower-blue eyes and spilled over.

He found his handkerchief and held it out to her awkwardly, and then as she didn't see it but stood there brushing the tears away like a child on her sleeve, he put his arm round her with clumsy gentleness and wiped them away himself.

'Damned if I can understand you, Sarah,' he said gruffly. 'I've never seen you cry before, and I don't like it . . . Dammit, it *upsets* me!'

This made her smile and she took the handkerchief from him and finished wiping her eyes herself. 'I'm sorry,' she said with a catch in her breath. 'I didn't mean to upset you, Tam. I won't do it again.'

'I hope you won't,' he said. 'Because I don't like it. I don't like to see any woman cry . . . and especially you, Sarah.' He frowned at her. 'It's all this talk of M. Estoban not coming back, I suppose, and then there's Mel's wedding next week, and damned nonsense of that sort. Weddings always upset women.'

'No,' she said. 'It wasn't Mel's wedding.' Romance, golden and glittering, and dying when you were only twenty-six. 'Oh my dear love,' sighed her heart, 'I'll never see you again . . .'

And then the door opened and James, guiltily playing truant, squeezed his small body round the door.

'Mamma!' he said. 'I want you.'

'Then you shall have me.' She knelt down and held out her arms and he ran into them and put his own shorter ones tightly round her neck. 'Why James,' she said caressingly, 'what did you want with me?'

'Only to tell you that I love you, Mamma!'

'Oh James,' she said. 'My dear little son!' The gold and glitter of high romance, surely it would fade in time under this warm, human contact? His father stared down at them both perplexed, and then he shouted, 'He's mine too, isn't he?'

They looked up in alarm but he was only pretending to frown. He stooped and picked the child up and lifted him easily on his broad shoulders. 'Now I'm going to give you a treat,' he said. 'You shall both come and tell me where I am to build my new stables!'

He was so large and strong that his left hand was enough

to hold the child safe, and having got him settled he held out his free hand to help his wife to her feet. Then, with a smile that pleaded with her for understanding, and a learning of the lesson of contentment that his deep and speechless love for her would teach her in years to come, he kept her hand in his and the three of them, bound together in a kind of quiet harmony, went down to the stable block together.

# Strangers In Company

## JANE AIKEN HODGE

A holiday coach tour – or a Greek Nightmare?

Marian and Stella were strangers when they met at the airport, ready to depart for Athens and their Mercury bus tour of Greece. Marian, plagued by bitter memories from the past, was nominally in charge of her young companion.
But this was no ordinary bus tour and their fellow travellers no ordinary holidaymakers. Haunted by death and danger, the two of them see their travelling companions struck down one by one, until at last it becomes a mere struggle for survival. But as the tension mounts against the ever-changing background of classical Greece, Marian and Stella become strangers no longer, but unite to face the dangerous nightmare of the world around them.

'A cliff-hanging climax brings this sharply-observed and well-told story to a happy ending'
*Sunday Telegraph*

'Enjoyable thriller with a picturesque background... the story builds up to a very exciting and unexpected climax' *Woman's Journal*

'All the lightness of Georgette Heyer and with added substance besides' *New Statesman*

# Horatia

## MARY ANN GIBBS

Horatia Pendleton stood to inherit a fortune when she came of age – if she lived that long. Her wicked uncle was plotting to marry her off to a friend or dispose of her in a more permanent fashion.

Reluctantly Horatia turned her back on Newcross, the only home she had ever known. In just four months' time she would be twenty-one and mistress of her fortune. In the meantime she must disguise herself and hope that her uncle wouldn't find her.

But Horatia, outspoken and independent, was never good at keeping quiet. Dashing Mr Latimer found that she irritated him exceedingly when he came to pay court to the sweet young daughter of the house. For there was Horatia, a runaway heiress, flouting the conventions by masquerading as a stableboy.

# The Penniless Heiress

## MARY ANN GIBBS

When the Brighton coach pulled into the Two Apprentices yard, Harriet Strangeways arrived in London. She was a red-haired little girl, travelling alone – and no-one came to collect her. In her broad country accent she told Martin that her uncle, Sir Everard Maltby, was supposed to be meeting her. And Martin, who hid a soft heart beneath his brash young man-about-town exterior, took pity on the child.

Martin had no way of knowing that, by offering Harriet shelter for the night, he was establishing himself as her guardian. Sir Everard refused to accept that she was the heiress to Maltby Cross and Harriet was put in the charge of Martin's formidable aunt, the Dowager Lady Eddicombe.

As the years passed, Harriet grew into a breath-taking beauty, whose rumoured fortune made her the talk of the town. But to Martin she was still just little Harriet Strangeways . . .

# HISTORICAL ROMANCE FROM CORONET

### MARY ANN GIBBS

| | | |
|---|---|---|
| ☐ 18984 3 | Horatia | 35p |
| ☐ 19349 2 | The Penniless Heiress | 35p |

### JANE AIKEN HODGE

| | | |
|---|---|---|
| ☐ 19906 5 | Strangers in Company | 40p |
| ☐ 10734 0 | Here Comes a Candle | 35p |
| ☐ 15029 7 | Marry in Haste | 30p |

### ALISON MACLEOD

| | | |
|---|---|---|
| ☐ 15885 9 | The Trusted Servant | 30p |
| ☐ 15807 7 | No Need of the Sun | 35p |

### JOCELYN KETTLE

| | | |
|---|---|---|
| ☐ 18813 8 | Memorial to the Duchess | 50p |

### NORAH LOFTS

| | | |
|---|---|---|
| ☐ 18403 5 | Nethergate | 40p |
| ☐ 16216 3 | Lovers all Untrue | 30p |

### ANYA SETON

| | | |
|---|---|---|
| ☐ 01951 4 | The Winthrop Woman | 40p |
| ☐ 02469 0 | Dragonwyck | 35p |
| ☐ 02488 7 | Foxfire | 35p |
| ☐ 17857 4 | Green Darkness | 50p |
| ☐ 15683 X | The Mistletoe and Sword | 30p |

*All these books are available at your bookshop or newsagent, or can be ordered direct from the publisher. Just tick the titles you want and fill in the form below.*

---

CORONET BOOKS, P.O. Box 11, Falmouth, Cornwall.

Please send cheque or postal order. No currency, and allow the following for postage and packing:

1 book—10p, 2 books—15p, 3 books—20p, 4–5 books—25p, 6–9 books—4p per copy, 10–15 books—2½p per copy, 16–30 books —2p per copy, over 30 books free within the U.K.

*Overseas* – please allow 10p for the first book and 5p per copy for each additional book.

Name .................................................................................

Address ...........................................................................

...........................................................................................

...........................................................................................

Miss Cheriton hoped that one of the young French officers on parole in Doverton would help to raise her dear niece's spirits after an unhappy love affair. But unfortunately Lieutenant Philippe Cadot was not interested in Melissa Prestwick. All his attention was held by the fascinating Lady Tamporley, still beautiful but married so young that she already had five children. And in the brief English spring a bittersweet romance blossomed between them.

Meanwhile fate was taking a hand in Melissa's affairs. The man she had jilted reappeared, courting another girl. And although Mel was still smarting from being taken for granted, her heart started to soften towards her former beau.

 CORONET BOOKS/HODDER PAPERBACKS LTD.

Fiction

ISBN 0 340 18985 1

| UNITED KINGDOM | 35p |
| AUSTRALIA | $1.10 * |
| NEW ZEALAND | $1.10 |
| CANADA | $1.25 |

*recommended but not obligatory